THE BOOK
OF SEI

David Brooks

faber and faber

LONDON · BOSTON

First published in 1988
by Faber and Faber Limited
3 Queen Square London WC1N 3AU
This paperback edition first published in 1989

Photoset by Wilmaset Birkenhead Wirral
Printed in Great Britain by
Richard Clay Ltd, Bungay, Suffolk
All rights reserved

British Library Cataloguing in Publication Data

Brooks, David
The book of Sei
I. Title
823'.914 [F]   PR6052.R581/

ISBN 0-571-15285-6

For Nikki and Jessica, again

Contents

Acknowledgements

The following stories have already been published in 1985 by Hale & Iremonger Pty Limited, Sydney, Australia, in *The Book of Sei and Other Stories*:

'The Book of Sei', 'The Dolphin', 'The White Angel of Mantria', 'Du', 'The Journal of Roberto de Castellán', 'Blue', 'The Lost Wedding', 'John Gilbert's Dog', 'Black', 'The Misbehaviour of Things', 'The Line', 'The Poet N.', 'Depth of Field', 'Striptease', and 'Roses'.

Acknowledgements are also made to the following publications in which some of these stories originally appeared: *Science Fiction* (1983) for 'The White Angel of Mantria'; *Urban Fantasies* edited by David King and Russell Blackford (Ebony Books, 1985) for 'Du'; *The Bulletin Literary Supplement* (1982) for 'Blue' and 'Black'; *Linq* (1985) for 'The Lost Wedding'; *New England Review/Bread Loaf Quarterly* (1984) for 'John Gilbert's Dog'; *Transgression* ed. Don Anderson (Penguin, 1986) for 'The Misbehaviour of Things'; *The State of the Art* ed. Frank Moorhouse (Penguin, 1983) for 'The Line'; *The Australian Literary Quarterly* (1987) for 'Sheep'; *Island Magazine* (1987) for 'The City of Labyrinths'; *Meanjin* (1987) for 'The Family of the Minister' and *Fine Line* (1987) for 'The Book'.

The Book of Sei

The Sei Mountains

This part of the country had been poorly mapped. One could guess why. The hills rose abruptly, tall and sharp as the columns at the outer gate of the palace, a forest of strange fingers rising from the plain, with a maze of uncharted trails winding between them, ascending into the mist that, at this late hour, thickened about the higher rocks and trees. The highway, a dim path barely three men broad, climbed with the valley floor through thick vegetation over stones worn smooth by an unsteady trickle of travellers to the south, refugees of hundreds, perhaps a thousand years, from the isolation and cold, the dark and lawlessness of the north. In the rift between mountains, under the heavy cover of the trees, the night came sooner than he had expected. He had passed no house or inn for two hours now, and could see none before him. He pressed forward, using his staff for soundings increasingly as the light faded, and grateful at last for the faintest shining from the stones. With no light, no clearing, no dry wood, he could make no fire to ward off the cold or the animals of these mountains.

He had almost resolved, none the less, to sleep out under the giant leaves when the overhang broke and he could see thousands of stars. In the space of a few paces the tangled vegetation gave way on the left to cropped shapes, and the wet, dark stones of the path to the hard white sand of a branching trail. He paused and looked about him. Starlight salted the leaves of the cassia. He could hear running water. Somewhere, deep in the forest behind him, he heard the crashing of a large animal, or of a bough falling. On a nearer bough he thought he saw the shape of an owl, silhouetted against the night sky.

He stepped along the trail. At its end was a small cottage, a thin light, honey-coloured, leaking between the planks of the door. He knocked. The wood, sweating, felt damp and grimy beneath his knuckles. Something, a cat, brushed against his calves and slipped inside as soon as the door opened. This it did slowly, and a woman's form appeared, backlit by a large candle on a table at the centre of a low, dark room. Her head was bare, and he could see that the green robes she wore were of an unusual quality. Throughout his introduction, explanation, and her cautious agreement to give him food, tea and directions to a lodging, her face remained in shadow. When he had entered, however, and been seated at the table, he saw a woman of beauty. He could see, as she placed roast fowl before him, and rice in a deep, black bowl, that her hands, though slim, were long-fingered and strong. When he glimpsed her eyes, as he passed her at the door or when she served him the clear, green tea, he thought they were large and deeply recessed, as of someone who suffered, or who worked long into the night. She was taller than most women, and had about her, in her hands, her face, her postures, that faint penumbra he had always thought the index of a sad wisdom, an involuntary accommodation of darkness.

She sat behind him as he ate, and they held a fragmentary conversation. She was a weaver. She kept a cat and other small animals. Yes, she had heard of the new wars northward, but wars were frequent there and she had seen, this time, few refugees. She had often fed them, when they came, and had thought he might be one of them. He asked, then, if she were a widow, if she had children. She remained silent. When he had finished eating, she told him of the next inn, a valley away, but that if he could leave her a little money, he could sleep in one of the two rooms at the side of the cottage; she would give him bedding. He agreed, thanked her in the name of the emperor and, declaring himself already weary, asked if he might retire immediately. He was shown to a small room with one gauze-covered window, open onto the night. There was reed matting on the stone floor and the walls were covered by green hangings into which were woven designs that glimmered gold and silver in the candlelight. She unrolled a thin mattress, covered it with white linen, and withdrew.

Tired as he has, he could not sleep. He lay staring at the pale rectangle of gauze over the window and the strange, silver trails on the tapestry. For the first time he noticed the humidity of the night, and the heavy, sweet exhalations of the earth. The air itself seemed a thick, viscous liquid, the grains of it like things alive and swimming in strange schools across his eyes. Through the thin wall he heard the continual soft *thuk* of the loom interspersed with the faint slide and whir of the shuttle. At one point he heard the scrape of a chair on stone, the sound of a cat. Much later, the sound of a heavy cloak falling, the sound of his own soft gasp as fingers trailed like leaves over the base of his belly.

They separated. In the moonlight from the window they were fish in a rock-pool. He would follow her into the shadow of ledges. He would fertilize her as she spawned. She leaned forward. Saliva stretched from her mouth, pooled in the centre of the sheet. He licked it, swallowed it all. They were earthworms. They were snails on a mountain path. They were ash trees. Sex was a shudder on the wind, a dispersal of seeds. They would make love days from now, miles distant, in the furrow of a field. Neither would know. He was a crab. He mouthed a dark anemone, an oyster, a pearl. Tentacles drew him closer as the hard beak reached for him, writhing in an inky cloud, finding no grip.

She changed. He did not. He was a separate consciousness, immutable. *She* was the bitch beneath him, back concaved, sex and anus thrust to him. A lizard, arms and legs splayed and angular, flat against the rock. A horse, the moonlight shiny on her flank. From the wall he saw them, from the ceiling. It was always a man's eyes, always a man's heart, always a human mind; the traveller and the sorceress, the lady of cats and pythons. Saurian monsters reared, clawing, gnashing in climax or death. The world filled with a distant murmuring, a growl, a

3

jungle shriek. Blood came, droplets of mucus, rose-coloured in the thin, dark hair of the cleft. He lay on his back, stretched upward, tasted, the giant stirring beneath tons of earth, the ash seed thrusting its tongue into the darkness skyward, breaking from a case of rock. *He* changed.

The Dog

In the dog, one of the simplest forms, she is on all fours, her back bent inward, her belly grazing the mattress, the skin from her haunches like a ski-slope, or the drift of a dune. His hands travel downwards to her shoulders or grip at her waist, leaving red pressure-marks, welts, five-fingered blushes. Penetration is deep. She is possessed, but lonely. High above her, his isolation is like an eagle's in that watch for prey that some mistake for power, or like an owl's in that sad insomnia so frequently confused with wisdom.

The Crab

She lies face down against the sheets, her arms bent before her like pincers, her legs splayed and buttocks raised slightly for penetration. He sits above her as if in a saddle. Penetration is slight and often awkward. She is restrained, or naturally passive. His urgency is expressed in short, sharp thrusts. Sensation is localized. They are familiar, isolated, perhaps tired: a creature of the beach and rock-pool, unwilling to enter the deeper water.

The Gulf

The night is a great maw, a gulf into which all his manifestations pour. He looks at her, as something below him thrusts deeply. The night drifts in a thick vapour between them. Through it, as through a dark, fogged window, he sees a pale blur, a mouth open in some cold, distant passion. The rictus of a drowned woman, suspended beneath the surface. Or *is* it the surface? Is that his own face?

Landscape

After love he grazes upon her body, the gully of her thighs, shoulders that in the moonlight are a silver field, her sweat not sweat now but a thin saccadic dew. Obscurely, ineffably, this explains the long beach and the wind-whipped sand, the women, far before him, dancing naked in a circle, their limbs flashing with the platinum light of a descending star. He can count easily the times that he has seen them. He approaches, but it is always like a wave, pulled back by the laws of moon and water. The wind drifts their cries to him in fragments. Sometimes there is a fainter music. That is where it ends: the cry, the sand stinging his calves, the taste of salt in his mouth.

Where she goes, or what she sees, he can never know. She tells him of a red meadow with a warm wind turning the mills. She tells him of a girl on a blue horse in a field of thick clover, the breeze licking her naked body like a lover.

The Vulture

This is a position much feared and maligned, although in truth it is very like a deer coming to drink at a forest pool, or like those great water-holes of the veldt at which at dusk the springbok and lion, elephant and hyena gather in their strange truce. She sits on her haunches, knees slightly apart, while he lies on his back before her, his legs parted and his buttocks high in her lap, his sex at her breast that she might tongue or fondle it as she desires. In this position neither is lonely – although loneliness, of course, is a supple companion. They are face-to-face, though their faces are far apart, and his sex is displayed between them. He must see what she does to him, while her sex remains out of his reach. He must give to receive. It is a position of conscious concord. This is why he is often afraid, and will call it the

Vulture. This is why, when he has overcome his fear, it is like the rare truce of the veldt. Alternatively, he is an altar for the sacrifice of himself. At the Zoroastrian platforms of the dead the vultures performed the function of high priests, lifting portions of the lifeless flesh into the heavens of Asia Minor.

Owl-blink/Cassia

She was a goddess, and will be again, that now has green eyes and the hide of a panther. What was he, that is now purely male? *A man*, he thinks. *Which of the shapes was that?*

Not the slightest shifting of air stirs the high trees. Mosquitoes sit motionless on the stone sill. An owl blinks, softer than the click of the cassia.

Birds and Death

In the first dream he entered the high, glass-domed conservatory of a great mansion, a room round and light-filled, with high walls of a dirty cream colour and hung at many levels with cages of a grey, weathered wood. At the centre of the floor, in the large circle where a garden had been, there was only bare earth, dry and hard-packed, dappled with bird-lime, a few short, dead stalks stubbling the surface. On the walls, and suspended from thin cross-beams, were open perches and swings, upon which, broken out from their cages, were a few birds of grey and brown colourings, some occasionally fluttering to a different vantage, some shifting on the wooden rods with a dry shuffle of their claws. All were silent; most were sleeping, or staring, as if ill or drugged, through dull eyes at vacant middle distances.

In the cages he discovered many more; some similarly catatonic, some dead. Several of the cages were overcrowded, others empty, and in many which at first appeared empty he found, in dark recesses, the small, huddled shapes of birds dead or dying. A few of the latter he held in his hands, staring into eyes that seemed incapable of any response but a dull, unshifting gaze.

There was no water. Small troughs and clay bowls lay about empty of

6

seed. With a methodical external calm that masked an interior frenzy he
began trying to rescue, to revive, to rehouse the overcrowded, to bring
water, to set the room in order. Vain from the start. A dusty light fell
about him. He felt exhausted even as he began. A stale place; a dirty stale
place of dryness and death.

The Phoenix

He lies on his back while she straddles him, her knees beside his
lower ribs, as if riding. As she raises and lowers herself, or rocks
back and forth, she controls the contact and the friction between
them. She may be thus either huntress or fox, riding in search of
her own brief death, or running to prevent it. Over and again she
may seek it only to escape it. Over and again he will find himself
wondering whether she is the phoenix, rising from the flames of
itself, or only the ghost of the phoenix, lost in a dark backcountry,
dreaming of resurrection.

Lobster, Scorpion, Lyre

Again, this is a form often feared, by her as by him, for its
implications of subservience and vulnerability. The fears are
false. She lies on her back with her legs apart; he lies or crouches
between them, his head at her sex. He begins as a reptile or
quadruped drinking at a pool. She begins as a pool. As she rises
towards climax she may seem a lobster upturned, or the scorpion
that stings itself in a slow, tensioned arc. In repose afterwards
they can be seen to have in fact been lyre-birds, unconscious of
their own beauty, fooled by their own mimicry. This is a transform-
ational form. Fearless, utterly uninhibited, it becomes the Cat.

The Snow-Owl

In this form he sleeps while she watches, lying propped upon one
elbow beside him. She may touch him, trailing her hand over his

belly and sex, eliciting unconscious translations into his dream or half-dream. If he wakes he sees that her pupils have the remote darkness of deep ice on a pool, that her irises are the rings of bare trees, that the whites of her eyes are snowfields, perhaps of a country in which he has just travelled. This form, like so many others, may be reversed, he watching while she sleeps. As he trails his hand over her breasts, her sex, her belly, he witnesses an occasional trembling or whimper as she wanders in a world that is partly of his own making, mostly utterly beyond it, the snow-owl, leaving its branches, flying back into its own landscape.

Language and Desire

Late at night, or late in an argument, when the talk has run its course and still 'possession' – of the thing talked about, or of each other – has proved impossible; when language, or the will and energy to use it, has been exhausted and the weight of what it cannot carry seems heaviest; then, it may be, they turn to the physical expressions of desire, as if to seek, in their penetrations, their surrenderings, to go where language cannot, as if the desire they feel is not something distinct from language, but a product, an inseparable part of it, and the need for physical satisfaction is in some way its extension. Becoming thus another kind of speech, the act of love becomes also a comment upon, and a mirror to, the world outside it, and yet the lovers, entering a place beyond words, can have no words with which to take what they find there back into the world they must eventually re-enter: the two worlds remain in this sense for ever apart, however linked, for ever linked, however much apart, each with its different language of desire.

The Dolphin

Half crab, half dog, her weight is supported on her shoulders, breast and knees. She may be at the edge of a bed, or fully upon

8

it. Penetration is deep, but slow and gentle. Supported similarly on knees and elbows he arches over her, and the curve of his spine is like that of the guardian creatures who pace us, several yards offshore, as we walk along deserted beaches in winter or late autumn. Below him she is the sea, although this, of course, should not deceive him, for she is also walking along the sand, looking out to where he threads the waves of their unconscious meeting.

In Australia, images of *Delphinus delphis* have been found in rock-caves deep in the heart of the desert, in a region thought to have once been a vast inland sea, and there are those in another hemisphere who say that the Delphic oracle was just such a creature before she became a woman – that the voice that warned Oedipus, that spoke to Leontes of Perdita, was the voice of the sea, speaking through that creature who swims beside us, the first artist, sewing wave to wave to a pattern beyond our conception.

The Plough

Her knees hooked over his shoulders, the clothes of the bed bunched to support her lower back, she seems a mill-wheel, a white hoop of stream water. Legs taut behind him, arms stiff to hold him above her, he is, it may be, the stream itself. Penetration in this position is deep and climax can be swift. Now, however, they move slowly and stay still for long periods, as if struggling to prolong the process – as if, in this protraction, they find some sort of comfort for obscure cruelties from which they have begun only now to realize they suffer. A mill-wheel and a stream, a stick and a hoop; but tonight, perhaps, they are like nothing so much as the mosquitoes on the sill beside them, motionless but for the occasional slow thrust of abdomen, the periodic trembling of moonlight on leaflike, transparent wings, or like the night sky beyond in which, sometimes, they might see a shooting star, a cloud pass over the constellation of the plough.

9

Birds and Water

There was a second dream, again of birds. He was again in a mansion, a different one, living in a room on the second floor. It had been an overcast day, and an afternoon of strange, immanent light, giving to everything a sharp, pearled freshness, rendering the wide front lawn a lustrous green, the white of the mansion whiter, the grey of its slate roof a richer grey.

He was about to go somewhere and went up to the room to change. He noticed, as he took clothes from his cupboard, that the air which circulated from the open window was restless, eerie, as if a storm were coming on. He went to the sill and stood at it to contemplate the weather. As he did so a bird flew in. When he turned, startled, to look at it, another did likewise, a robin, the scarlet of its breast contrasting dramatically with the emerald-green of the first as they perched, only centimetres apart, on the bookshelf. Others came and perched on the chair-back, the shelves of the open cupboard. He moved to the door and stood watching as the room became a strange, almost silent aviary. Birds continued to arrive, of many colours and sizes. He remarked particularly the three owls that perched on the outer edge of the bed, in order of size descending towards him; a large grey owl, a smaller grey and white, a smaller red and grey. When he looked back to the window he saw that more birds had caught in the lace curtains and clung there, looking out to the sky behind them. Others were perched on the window-ledge or on the narrow desk before it.

As if at some particular signal – perhaps at the first drops of rain – the birds began to fall where they perched. Not all of them, but many. The first he saw do so were those on the curtains: they simply hung there, upside-down, as if they had died in a trap. Then those on the bed began to topple, those on the chair-back. Again he came close to panic and rushed to revive them, expecting again helplessness, death. But now, in this luminous dusk, they awoke with a suddenness that astonished him. He had merely to place his hands about them and they stirred, struggling to right themselves, white birds, blue birds, emerald-green birds, perching as before, watching the now teeming rain.

The Eagle

As in the Dog, her knees and elbows are to the mattress. He lies or crouches behind her, his mouth to her sex that is like an inverted exclamation-mark, or a ravine with a dark star above it. His tongue can enter her deeply. He is blind, and has taste only. This too is a lonely form, though its loneliness is that of the child. His penis will become erect and hard against the sheets. It is she who is the eagle. He plunges deep into a black water. He may become lost, but for him it is now a condition without fear or division.

The Fish

Mouthing at first the tendons of her inner thighs, tonguing the creases at the edges of her sex, the hairs that stand above it like dark reeds, he approaches her clitoris in ever-narrowing circles, like ripples rebounding from the rim of a pool. He wades inward, breaking at last into slow, fluid strokes as the bank slips from him and he makes for that place where he can tread water or sink, feeling beneath him the warm upsurge of a deeper spring. He is, in this, the swimmer, she the pool, though of course they may be reversed. He lies on his back, she crouches beside him, and takes his penis in her mouth. As she repeatedly tongues, engulfs and withdraws it, the waves of increasing sensation spread outward in widening circles over his belly and thighs. He becomes the pool, she its only occupant, and what light there is is submarine, the rippled bedclothes sinews of a deeper sea. They are less creatures than place, less place than creatures containing it. They move as fish seen from the surface, the light's play and diffraction making them indistinct, beings that are and are not separable from their medium. Each can be a fish within a pool, a pool within a greater being, indeterminate within the wider waters of the night.

The Bowl

Black on a black background, as if struggling in darkness, or just emerging from it, finely smoothed and polished by the

11

craftsman so that they slide sensuously, seductively beneath the fingers, all manner of animals are arranged about it, a complex interlace of beasts. To see them properly, to discern their detail, one must look closely, turning the object slowly in the light. One sees then that they are endlessly connected, that their circle is perpetual, a dog linked by the teeth to a stag's leg, a snake twisted about the wing of an eagle, others linked at teat, vulva, phallus, as if attempting bizarre miscegenations. Several of the faces are obscured. Of those that are visible, some have been given human features. One cannot tell whether the expression upon them is of pain or pleasure. Nor, at last, can one tell whether it is the bowl that holds them together, or they the bowl.

The Plough

In this position they cannot kiss without effort. For each it is easier to study, across a small bridge of darkness, the weather of the other's face. They are gentle, unhurried, undemanding: he can see, as the wave rises within her, the way she turns her head, the way she bites the knuckle of her clenched right hand; she can watch, as his eyes close and his face contorts, the reserve that seems so characteristic of him collapsing into childlike urgency.

Time, that has already dilated to allow their meeting, has opened so far now that seconds become like hours, minutes like days or weeks. They can sometimes see, in the duration of this as in other pairings, a deeper change, a deeper shift of season or emotion. The stream flows but remains always the same stream; the water-wheel turns but goes nowhere: in this act, this mating, they have each been profoundly present, and yet also away, in the far fields of themselves, surveying, it may be, the devastation, but aware also of possibilities of tillage, of further growth. Like the imagos that abound in the night around them, they are at once delicate and have the shape and patina of monuments, the movement and intensity of forces far greater than themselves.

The Leopard

He begins slowly, at a man's pace through the veldt, the stands of low trees. The air is heavy with near-dusk. It is languid and moves over him like a thin sea. Somewhere giraffes graze upper branches. At some point, moving towards a water-hole, wildebeest disect in a lazy diagonal a basin in the savannah. The sinews of his forelimbs, the fur on his shoulders, ripple about him and shimmer in the still, watery eyes of gazelles who stare passively as he passes, seeing from his gait and eyes' fixedness that his prey is other, is still some way off. Gradually his speed increases, he begins to lope. The dust rises gently behind him. He notices less now, his eyes focused on an invisible, racing point some five or six yards before him, choosing his path as rapidly as he, now running, devours it. Thin legs flash in panic from his field of vision: though he does not see them, flocks of birds rise from the trees, an elephant is startled and crashes through the brush, the flight of smaller animals creates a strange wake in the grasses behind him. Now in smoother, more open country, he moves yet faster, his paws marking the ground more lightly and at wider intervals, that slow rocking beginning within him that marks his highest speed, his body now a wave barely grazing the ground beneath him. Suddenly there is a wheel, an arc in the air, a panting, a lusting as he tears, the spat of blood in his nostrils, the rip of skin and hair. Ripples, large at first, spread out in the plain, disappear at last, and faintly, into the far trees.

I was there: there were two of us. The prey we caught was our own sorrow. Our loneliness. What a feast it was!

The Cat

She lies on her back, her weight on her neck and shoulders, her knees, slightly apart, pulled to her chest and held there by him as he crouches before her. In this way he can rock her, sweeping with his tongue an arc from her anus to above the hood of her clitoris. They appear to have the shamelessness of the cat that tends it hindquarters in full view of its human, but individual prides have been abandoned for the true pride of the cat in its cleanliness. They are one animal. It washes itself.

Terracotta

He lies on his back, legs flat to the sheets, arms relaxed or stretching out to where his fingers touch the soft flesh of her hips. Her back to his gaze, she squats upon him, controlling her penetration, free to watch it more closely. Each is alone, although both drift with a current that is like a greater law, a greater swimmer, aiming for a shore that neither can foresee. He cannot watch her face, cannot tell whether her expression is of wonder or of weeping, nor if the grimace to which it rises is of pleasure or of pain. In truth it is more than this, the part-animal, part-human face of a pre-Columbian terracotta of the earth mother, bearing down in the act which creates her. Pinned by her ankles, by the weight of her hands, he is denied the active search for his pleasure, reduced to a state of helpless anticipation, as if, accustomed to thinking himself its progenitor, its distant precursor, he is now the site and product of an act of birth, present, abandoned, unforearmed.

The Child

Part lynx, part dog, part owl, part almond tree, part gryphon, part phoenix, part dolphin, part vulture, part wanderer, part sorceress, part son daughter of an actress and a Chinese clerk, part poet, part weaver, part exile in the late twentieth century in the remotest city of the remotest continent of the world. Part fish, swimming the dark tunnels, part the cave at the end of the swimming. Part sperm, part ovum. Part a tongue, shaping sounds from the wind, part wind. The sex within the sex. The creature within the landscape. The landscape within the creature within the white ripples of starlight that Wu Lei remembers as he writes to a woman in a far province, to ask

14

whether she is with child, the uncountable rays of the moon reaching the round earth south of Mount Shan, salting the leaves of the cassia, making the world.

The Sei Mountains (II)

The light that poured through the gauze at the window stung his eyes. The heat of it scoured him. The slack breeze of a mid- or late morning chafed invisible bruises. Already the warm shifting air had dried their juices, coating his sex with a thin, glistening membrane. An ovum. An egg glaze. As he turned onto his back he felt their moisture in the creases of his groin, cool as the air touched it. He placed his hand there, pressing his fingers deeply into his scrotum, and brought them to his face to smell for her. Warm, acrid, animal, she was still there, and would be for days yet, deep in the pores, the folds of loose skin. His penis stiffened and he lay there, a long time, his body focused about that centre, trying to recapture something of his changes, the feel and thrust of her, the planes of her flanks and belly in the moonlight, the sharp, hot odour of her sex. When at last he rose, it was awkwardly, on unsteady legs and a back set in sleep, an imago emerging from the night of the chrysalis, a new foal struggling to stay upright. Through all the metamorphoses of the night there had been a deeper change. His mind seemed now untried, his life before this a constricting skin now somewhere in the dark behind him. He struggled to remember the journey, the message, an owl's eyes, a path to this door.

Upright, leaning on the sill, he tried to remember her face, to compose himself to words he could offer when he met her. The window opened on a small, grassed clearing hedged by forest. Geese and a few chickens pecked at corn the colour of old gold, spilling from a wooden pail that lay on its side beside a bush of scarlet berries. Swallows cut the air between the forest and the house. Small lizards, a deep onyx-green, basked on a low stone wall that ran down one side of the clearing and crumbled into a pile of smooth river-stones.

15

She was not there. Nor, having dressed in a loose robe he discovered folded beside the bed, could he find her in the dark house or amongst the sculptured shrubbery before it. The white quartz of the front path glistened in the sunlight. A cat woke and stretched on its back when he opened the heavy door. He went back to his room and waited some time for the sounds of her. At last, hungry, he went into the kitchen and found there milk in a porcelain jug, bread, fresh vegetables, eggs in a stoneware bowl. A crock of rice, already cooked, stood spiced and aromatic at the centre of the wooden table, beside chopsticks and a painted cup. A dark crock – the black, figured crock of the night before.

She did not return – at least, not evidently, and not to him. Each morning for three days he found the grain renewed on the lawn, the milk replenished in the porcelain jug, bread in a new loaf, the cat seemingly fed and unconcerned. But the cloth on the loom progressed no further, and although, from the eyes of the cat, a swallow, one of the geese or lizards, she might have been watching him, he caught no further glimpse of the woman. By the third day, as if a drug were leaving his bloodstream, he had begun to doubt whether he had seen her at all. The morning scent on his fingers had grown fainter, become instead that of things he had touched since her leaving – mandarins, oil, the wood of the table, stones, the black earth, cassia leaves.

That evening the cat leapt onto the table as he ate. It made no attempt to approach his food, and he did not brush it away. It sat at arm's length and stared past him at the movement of their shadows cast on the wall by the lamplight. When he had finished his rice he watched it, determined at last to discover whether she had taken that form, whether she had been with him all that time. Eventually it turned to him and they gazed at one another. Its eyes, at first as dark and strange as some cold star, became increasingly familiar, the glaucous eyes of the snow-owl, a grey-blue like that of the sea at twilight. In the black slits at their centres he saw, however, only the double reflection of himself, faint stars of candlelight dancing in his own dark eyes. It was a mistake, a blind, to think so much had turned about her.

16

On the fourth day, very early, he left, taking the narrow highway to where it joined the greater. Only yards from the white path he saw, or thought he saw, a small, bright bird of a colour he had not seen before. When he looked to follow it he could find it nowhere. After walking half an hour, and still in the forest, he came to an area of cleared land. The morning mist had not yet fully risen, and wisps still lay on the sloughs. To his left, and slightly above him, on a rise in the green meadow, a white mare seemed to watch him, although as he stopped to look at it, it turned and cantered out of sight as if evanescence had been its very purpose – as if its deliberate point had been to emphasize, by going, the chill and eerie vacancy of which he now became so suddenly conscious, and which now hastened his steps away.

By mid-afternoon, in the next valley, and engaged already by the familiar commerce of the highway, he was beginning with difficulty a life in most appearances a resumption of the former. This, at least, is one of the endings, for some a more comfortable alternative to the wilderness of animals, imagos, that it otherwise becomes, the darkness of these letters valleys, or the bars of cages, where once was a firm white wall – owls, leopards stirring, where only a man had been.

The Fish

Dawn comes and defines the river. In pipes, basins, shower-stalls, the day begins with water rushing upon us, its darkness gone. Over coffee or the newspaper we enter its greater channels, mapping the backwaters, the currents that at night have no boundaries. We hear news from other hemispheres. We feel it in the air about us. The fish have sought the stream-bed, the slackpools that the current overpasses. They remain visible only to those who, in the midst of the stream, can pause, take a face in their hands, and look into the eyes for the far-off lights. The far-off, incessant flashing of bronze or silver.

The Tree

Loving, but not 'in love', she takes him to her bed. In this there is no indication of desire. An arrangement. They sleep like spoons, her breast at his back, her head behind his shoulder. He asks for her hand and she gives it. As she sinks further into sleep, or furls against the cold, it will be withdrawn. He knows this, and is kept awake by his longing. In the deep pit of her dream she is touching a stone. It may be the grave of their desire. He cannot reach it. His body is a dark tree. Pruned, it will bring forth fruit that is ripe and without bitterness. Unanswered, it is a slow, wild growth, overreaching its boundaries, bowed with a small, sour fruit. This is not her concern. It is his desire; it will wither and be contained by seasons more ancient than either of them has known. He remembers the way she has craved him. Now, cradling his own flesh in unexpected bitterness, he craves her in a way she does not recognize. When next he is invited to her bed he will face the usual difficult decision. And he will go.

Language and Desire

Never comprehended, never fulfilled, the relationship between them would go on, continue beyond any foreseeable bounds, a sentence in an unknown language, a symptom of something larger working itself out within them, completing and understanding itself even through their own incompleteness and incomprehension. Many although they remained one, one though they changed so often, their entwinings, their shapings and re-shapings would continue in places far from there, manifold reincarnations of that unfinished moment, movements of their sign through all its languages. Adequate knowledge, adequate description were impossible. Any attempt to name, to register, to represent them would bear a relation to their true shape like that of the cracked shell of a lobster, the heaped bones of a tiger, to the creatures that once they were part of.

The Lynx

He sits on a high, wooden balcony in a thin pool of light, the suburb dark in the foreground and beyond it the distant lights of the city, blue and white and yellow by the river. There is an empty cup beside the cane chair. A book. All he hears, when he listens, are the crickets and the traffic on the thoroughfare. A breeze from the sea winds over his arms and face in gentle, almost tangible cords, producing a rare, purely sensual pleasure. He stares out in utter silence, as if only his bones are dreaming. The breeze stirs the pages at his feet. A scent rises from the hibiscus. *She is here*, he realizes, putting his hand down, touching the ghost of a lynx.

Revenants

Throwing back the twisted sheets, he rises and goes to the window, holding his sex in his hand. He leans out above the hibiscus, sifting the night air for a dog's bark, the wooden shudder of a cart, anything by which he might lift himself further from his dream, the breasts searing his hands, the cleft scalding, the strong mouth stealing his breath. Slowly, steadily, he draws deep lungfuls of air. The sweat dries on his chest. Soon, numb, or drugged with stars, he will return to his bed. For a time he will sleep. For a time, banished by the lesser satieties that he will now search out, she will not visit him.

The Sei Mountains (III)

The light poured through the gauze at the window, waking him at last with its heat and intensity. He rose and, wrapping the robe loosely around him, moved out into the quiet of the lightless house. It was the fourth day; all seemed darker, chillier than it had been. The food was there as usual, but for the moment he ignored it, instead moving slowly about the inner rooms as he had done before, examining the furniture and

19

hangings in the dimness, deep in thought. After some time he moved back towards the room in which he had been sleeping. He held the window-gauze aside to glance out at the yard, its by now familiar objects for these few seconds preternaturally bright. Carefully, unhurriedly, he tore down the gauze, then turned to the room's embroidered hangings. These, their hunt scenes fragile in the stronger light, he pulled down likewise to expose the thin partitions that they covered. Kicking through one of these, he entered the studio and tore the warp of the unfinished fabric from the loom, stepping thence into the rest of the house and tearing down methodically its curtains and its tapestries. Light flooded in from windows he'd not seen before, gleaming from the porcelain, exposing the dust on the polished wood. Amidst the bars of this new light, through motes that filtered from the rent and fallen fabrics, he turned now to the table and the food, upending all with one strong motion of his arm and knee. The black crock broke into three large pieces, spilling its thousand grains in a broad, gibbous moon. For a second, it seemed, before he turned away, the animals on the broken pieces gnashed at each other in a last attempt to keep their taut, still circle whole.

Out in the yard he took off the loose robe and lay naked in the grass, bathed in sunshine. For a long time it must have seemed to the animals about him that he slept, though in truth he lay with eyes open, staring upward as if entranced by the light's play in the maples, or the way the faint breeze shifted their leaves.

Late in the afternoon, towards the false dusk that such valleys impose, he left, taking the narrow highway to where it joined the greater. Only yards from the path of crushed white quartz he saw, or thought he saw, a small, bright bird of a shape and colour he had not seen before. He looked to follow it but could not find it in the growing gloom. The shadows swallowed it as easily as they seemed to have done the house he had left. After walking half an hour, still in the forest, he came to an area of cleared land where the light seemed slightly stronger. To his left and just above him on a rise in the green meadow, a white mare seemed to watch him, its coat taking on a cold, lunar blueness in the dusk. As he stopped and bent to place his parcel on the ground, it took a pace or two towards him. Carefully, as if premeditatedly, he gathered a handful of stones from the path and, straightening, began to throw them at it one by one, moving towards it, bending to gather larger stones, not wondering as it stood staring through their approaching rain, and only relieved, when at last it cantered off, to hear some of the largest and the heaviest thwack loudly on its flank. Only relieved, to hear sobbing as his knees sank into the wet earth.

The Dolphin

It's not, I suppose, if I'm to tell the whole truth, that I'm completely the man I was, but in all of us there is some part that has lasted, some part that is still the same, and in some of us – like myself, and like Calvin, who is still as always my teacher – it is the part that remembers.

He writes to me that his last, great library, his monastery in the southern Tyrol, has been gutted by fire, and that now, in the senescence of his memory, he is having the greatest difficulty in recalling certain developments of the earliest times. Do I remember Angelica? I once spent much time with her. Only I can help him reconstruct the sequence of events, the story of the rain. The other day (it must be months gone now) he was walking out by the sea, to which he had travelled, after so many years in the mountains, for a rest, a cure while his home was reconstructed. The gulls were wheeling around him, shrieking their fragment of a language he is certain he once knew. At the end of the beach, at the tip of the rocky head, he heard, when the gulls had gone, an intermittent chirruping, and realized that it was the sound of dolphins as they surfed perilously near the rocks, disappearing at the last to resurface, long seconds later, far out amongst the breakers, beginning their game again. As if aware of something stirring within him, trying to answer them as he had been trying to answer the sea-birds, they then followed him all the way back to his cabin, two miles down the beach. Three times in the one week this happened to him: do I know what it means? do I remember the languages?

How can I begin? It will be easier, certainly, to write to Calvin than to tell someone who had not been there, for how could I explain that there was once a time when time did not pass as it does now, when those of us who were there then had the patience of stones, when days as we now know them – so long, as always, to the young – were for the first and oldest of us like the fleeting shadows of the clouds that now race across the sun, or like that click of one leaf on another that we cannot now separate, when the wind blows, from the continual soft whisper of the universe? Days now I have wandered the shore – for, unlike Calvin, I have lived by it always – and I have thought of nothing but the rain and the things that changed us. Sadly, all the songs are like elegies now, even our own. I no longer understand the chirrup of the dolphins, though once I did, and though I have long thought to tell the story of the birds, that too is now beyond me. Only the strongest memories have survived.

It's not – to get down to it – that our landing here was planned, or even by choice. It's simply that, in the rush to leave before our planet broke up, our craft was built hastily and not very well, and that, after so long looking for a home, we had eventually to land on the nearest object when we could no longer withstand the drift of the tiny meteors, the eroding cross-winds of space. Coming through the atmosphere was easier then, like sinking into a sauna, though the landing itself, with the craters and pot-holes and mud-pools, was difficult and broke up our craft. We all survived, and picked ourselves up, but there was hardly a scrap of the ship left. From then on we just had to make do.

At that time this planet was only beginning. We were lucky that there was anything to land on at all. It was still by and large a great ball of gases and magma, just starting to cool. Had we not crash-landed on one of the first hard bits we may never have survived. For a long time the ground was so hot that we hopped around rather like fleas, trying to spend less time touching the surface, developing thick calluses on our feet and moving constantly from one part of the crust to another to avoid the volcanoes that were always buckling it. As the planet spun further through space, of course, the surface cooled and the crustal plates thickened, coming at last to hold the red-hot centre like an eggshell holds a yolk, the surface then cooling all the faster and the atmosphere of steaming gases beginning to condense, preparing the rain.

23

In all this time – I can't say how long, for with only the heat, the gases, and the edible grey doughy stuff that somehow formed in them, there was little to help mark the passage of time – we did multiply somewhat, and small groups of us, as squabbles broke out in the boredom, spread out to occupy areas far from one another. We kept in touch for a while, letting each other know of a birth or a death, but as deaths amongst us were rare, and births, in all that barrenness, quickly came to be discouraged, we soon lost contact completely and lived our own separate lives. At the time I want to tell about – the time I remember most vividly – there were seven of us in a low place (though we did not know it then) on that side of the globe we now call the Pacific. These seven belonged to two families – mine, and that of my Uncle George. On my side there were my brother Calvin, my foster-sister Cora and myself. On the other there were George and Aunt Isabel, their daughter Angelica, and their adopted son Ralph, with whom I never got along.

Angelica then was one of the happiest creatures I have known, and her imagination and sense of humour were all, sometimes, that got us through our most boring periods without bickering or open warfare. She was lithe and very beautiful, with long silver hair, and I know that, until I usurped his claim, my mother and father for a long time nursed a hope that she might make a wife for Calvin, if he could pause long enough in his calculations to look at her.

Calvin was the brilliant one, though he didn't speak much, and for much of this period, observing his writings, his perpetual tabulations, we all rather naturally assumed that he was working on plans to get us away from this place. I used to go off with him on some of his interminable walks, and he would tell me – slowly of course, and always in fragments – about our history in the other place, and about the heavens we had travelled through. Later I was to discover that, along with his diaries and systems of navigation, it was this that he had carved into the rocks in his invented signs, so that he would never forget. Even now, all over that part of the globe, people are finding, in caves, on rock-faces, or carved into granite tors, fragments in one or another of his languages: snippets of our

24

ancient history, or star-guides, or maps of one or another of the landscapes that have been written again and again on that region since we got there.

Unlike my parents, who had aged considerably during our long flight and had died before our landing here, Uncle George and Aunt Isabel had retained all their old vigour and good temper. He was a big, big man who was always smiling under his great moustaches, and who had a laugh and a singing voice that could be heard valleys away. No one could understand how, with nothing to eat but the doughy stuff that condensed at dawn from the sulphurous clouds, he could have stayed so fat, for he spent no more time than the rest of us in the gathering that served as our only real occupation. Even during the beginning of the great rain, when he and his family caught their fabulous colds, he and Isabel were almost always to be found sitting off somewhere amongst the rocks, involved in one of their endless discussions as to the meaning of one or another of the portents she was for ever discovering, or divining from her star-disks, now so often handled and so worn that only she could guess what their faded figures meant. She was our High Priestess, I suppose, though of a religion only she much held or understood, for all her meandering attempts to persuade us in the long, steamy evenings as we watched the deep red sun set through the gas clouds.

Cora was only a child at this time, and spent most of her days playing in the warm mud, going on walks to different parts of the basin, or sitting listening to Angelica's stories. My cousin Ralph I would rather not talk about, though I suppose I must, if only for the sake of the other, darker side that was even then a part of everything. He was a difficult individual, and spent a lot of time brooding, wanting always to be in charge, resenting that there was not more to be in charge of. He was, it's true, important to us – curious and useful – but he shifted around like a thin, sharp shadow, an irritation at the edge of my brain.

I have thought a lot, in all the time I've had, upon the possible sources of Ralph's bitterness, but I have never been able to find a final cause. Who knows with what argument or misunderstanding, and with whom, it may have begun in that remote furrow of time before our being here began? Perhaps there were old wars, old enmities of which Calvin never knew. Certainly there were questions about the break-up of our planet to which neither he nor any of the others would provide sufficient answers, and to which now his memory will not extend. For a while I thought Ralph was merely jealous over Angelica, though as time went on this became less and less plausible. There seemed instead some gnarled edge, some burr, some hurt at his core that had come in time to trouble every fibre of his being – as if, perhaps, some greater law separated us, giving to all our misunderstandings the sense of something far deeper. In any case, he argued a lot at this time with Calvin and me, chiefly because we did not keep a greater watch on the other groups, and because we did not seem very concerned with how much of the bare, brown planet they might be taking over.

In the end the rain took care of that anyway. It happened slowly, a kind of natural progression as the Earth consolidated further. First came a time when the atmosphere thickened, a time of air increasingly heavy with steam, and then, as the outer layers of gas grew cooler in the chilly stellar night, an aeon of hot mists. Gradually, almost imperceptibly, our visibility was reduced until one had to move only a few short paces to be lost in the fog, and could tell relative positions by sounds alone – Uncle's wheeze, Ralph's mumbling, the drone of Isabel's prognostications, the cheeky, conspiratorial laughter of Angelica and Cora. Ralph, of course, thought this densening of the atmosphere a plot of those we'd not kept watch upon, while Calvin, lost in his writings, seemed not much to notice nor to care. And through it, day by day, there was Angelica, playing with my sister, or moving, a silent, silver apparition, through the thick white cloud.

In time the rain began, or rather, we found ourselves oppressed by that climatic condition that we now call rain, though this rain, the Great Rain, was both hot and perpetual, a condition we had to endure without relief for a time that would now seem incredible. With it, our visibility improved just slightly, and we began to move about naked, for our skin seemed better suited to the new conditions than the now tattered robes we had brought with us from the other planet. We had always made some use of the caves that the continual settling and reshaping of the land created, and we now began to live in them much of the time – or rather, Calvin, Cora and I, for while the perpetual downpour seemed to make us sluggish and anxious for comfort, it seemed only to make Ralph, Angelica and their parents livelier, as if the continual walls of falling water appealed to something deep within them as nothing on this oppressive planet ever had before. Even Uncle George, who suffered so badly from his cold at this time, found a new lease of life in the downpour, and his merriment as he wandered in it became as much a fact of life as the water. His whole family began to range further and further, and while I would accompany Angelica as often and as far as I could tolerate, it was always only to marvel jealously at the grace and ease with which she negotiated the mudslide and stoneslick, or swam in the pools and lakes and little seas that formed constantly about us.

Some time after the start of the rain, her half-brother – to my content, if not to that of his parents – disappeared on what came to be known as Ralph's Long Walk. He had talked for some time of setting out to find those he now termed our enemies, and after he had been gone a lengthy period it was naturally hoped that this was the reason for this absence. It was at about this time, moreover, that Uncle George's sore throat got worse, and that his problem seemed to spread to the rest of his family. Some time after the rain first came, he had begun to suffer from his persistent cold – not of a kind to make him miserable, or even particularly uncomfortable, but a continual cough, a dull pain in the throat, and a kind of anxiety that would not let him remain still or indoors for long. And now, first Isabel and then Angelica began to complain of strange sensations at the back of the neck or below the jaw, and these at last became so much a fact of their lives that, although they continued throughout Ralph's absence and for ages after his return, we soon ceased to ask after them or to comment upon the strange lumps that had appeared at the tops of their spines. It was not until one night in the cave when, my uncle and his family having been out in the rain some days, Calvin commented upon the strangeness of these developments, that I realized how uncharacteristic they were of our race.

The downpour continued. When Ralph returned, it was, after the jubilation of his parents subsided, to give us disturbing news. Not only had he found no trace of others, but he had made some remarkable discoveries. He had found a place where the land disappeared under a body of water so great that he could not see across it. He had tried to walk around it, but could find neither an end nor a significant curve to its shore. At last, after a long, long journey beside it, he had decided to return, and as he walked back – using, as we all now did, Calvin's systems of wind- and light-navigation – he had come upon what seemed to him, and soon to us all, the only possible explanation. Just as we had seen the lakes and small seas building in the valleys and recesses of the plains around us, so it must be that there were, in some places on this planet, vaster recesses, deeper valleys which, as they filled, would create greater and greater seas. These, it must be, were the places to which the waters of the endless rain were going, the eventual destination of all its runnels, rivers and torrents. As long at it rained the great seas must become even greater, taking more and more of the land in their expansion. If the rain did not stop – and who could say now that it would? – it might be that all of the land would be swallowed. And what, then, would become of us, stranded without hope of rescue on the most desolate, and now most treacherous of planets? And alone, by the looks of it; the last survivors of our race: for who could say that the other groups had not perished already in the flood?

Although we all discussed this a long time and earnestly, and although we moved to higher and higher ground, in truth the rising of the waters seemed to worry some of us more than others. And if Angelica would often come at my request to sit long periods in the drier caves, they were longer for her than for me, for she had come, like the rest of her family, to regard the teeming rain and the rivers and lakes it produced as almost as much her natural home as the sheltered places my family chose – for Calvin now spent all his time where the rain would not wear away his writings, and even Cora had forsaken Angelica's company for places where her own miniature mudscapes would not be flooded like the great one outside. Again and again, as I watched my cousin's sleek, silver form rise and melt into the outer world, I felt that the rain and all it had brought was forcing us apart, would turn the depth of feeling between us into a thinner and thinner tie that must eventually snap, for all the strength of our promises.

Ralph was now away most of the time, making expeditions to the outer waters, returning to tell us how far they had come. At last even we, on those short excursions to which our distaste for the water now restricted us, could walk towards where it gnawed at the edge of the land, and we realized that what had once been for us a whole, hot, steamy world had shrunk, not merely to a continent, but to one small and ever-diminishing island.

It was at this time that Aunt Isabel at last revealed her family's secret, a secret that not even Angelica, in our great intimacy, had passed on to me. For a long time they had been gone from us for greater and greater periods, and we now heard that these had been spent, not weaving between land and water as we had thought, but living entirely in the latter. They had entered at first for short periods only – an hour, a morning, a day at a time – but soon found that with practice they could hold their breaths for extraordinary intervals – that Ralph, having developed an even stranger faculty, could actually 'breathe' underwater. For longer and longer periods now, they could survive without need of land. The water had at last soothed the long pain in their throats, and the atmosphere of the surface was coming to seem to them increasingly thin, anxious and turbulent when compared with the calm, silent world beneath it. Uncle George confirmed it: he and Isabel, Ralph and Angelica had long been training against the time, which they were sure was fast approaching, when the land would disappear entirely beneath the waves. They had delayed their disclosures in the knowledge that we had not developed the same abilities as they, and in the hope that the rain might miraculously stop and that time never arrive when we would have to part.

And yet arrive it did. The waters continued to rise, the rain showed no signs of abating, and, their admission once made, Uncle George and his family now spent so much time in the water that their land-time became increasingly uncomfortable to them. Even Angelica found herself caught up in a process she could do nothing to reverse. For my sake, it is true, she spent more time on land than any of her family, but with each visit I found the time grew shorter and shorter before a trembling, a tiredness, an unsteadiness in her breathing signalled once again that I should walk her to the edge of the rising water, embrace her in the shallows, and let her go to them. Time, and changes which neither of us could understand, were separating us irrevocably. There came a day when her agony on land could no longer be tolerated, and I knew that she must die if she were to come to me again, just as I must if I were to enter for too long her new and impossible medium. She left for the last time, weeping, yet quickening to the touch of the warm salt liquid, hovering within sight until the last light had gone.

The rain ceased, and so soon as to seem deliberately to mock us. There was at first a general yet scarcely perceptible thinning in the downpour, and then, only a short time after Angelica's departure, the first breaks in the cloud, the first floodings of a light stronger and more pure than we had ever experienced before. Tiny, glimmering patches swept over and about us, tantalizing us with brief, accompanying pauses in the drizzle. And at last there came a whole day of brightness. From our peak the visibility seemed endless. Unhampered even by drifting showers, we saw the reaches of the planet as we had never seen them before, and with what a mixture of emotions! For we not only received for the first time a true sense of the smallness of our island and of how narrow our escape had been (but for a few distant summits like our own we could see about us nothing in any direction but water), but also, just beyond the white crests of the breaking waves, at a point close by, but which the rain had always obscured, we could see a lithe, sleek-headed silver shape threading the water, and beyond her – accompanied, whenever the breeze blew hard enough in our direction, by a still-familiar singing – a larger shape, doubtless moustachioed, waving, splashing to catch our attention.

From this point on things began to change rapidly. Almost before we knew it, the grey, doughy stuff that had been sustaining us, instead of dissolving in the steam and rain as it had always done, and left now to behave as it might always have planned, took root in rock-crevices and deposits of mud from still-active volcanoes, and began to take strange new shapes which Calvin identified as fungiform, lichenous. Soon there were mosses, minute insects, tiny plants with the fleshy leaves of aloes. We had seen none of these before, and yet had somehow seen all, for all, while so different from those of the place we had come from, were also so much the same – obeyed, as Calvin was soon to suggest, the same laws of system, the same evolutionary biases. Could it have been that we had somehow brought all of this with us? Could it have been that minute life-forms, spilling from our disintegrating spacecraft, had been inactive all these years, or, producing at first only the doughy grey stuff, had developed no further until the climatic conditions approached more nearly those of the planet we came from? Or could it simply be that life, wherever it happens, follows always the same unchangeable principles?

Larger plants came, small bushes, trees, and one day, from over the waters, a flock of big white birds, so strange, so beautiful, so utterly miraculous that it seemed to us that others of our race *had* survived – that, just as Uncle George and his family had become creatures wholly of the sea, so others of us must at some time have taken to the air. But how, if this were so, could they have survived the great rain? Perhaps there were places where it had not rained, or mountain-tops so high that they had been above the perpetual cloud. It was Calvin, of course, who brooded most upon these things, and who was least surprised at all that the birds seemed to promise. We must move, he said; we must gather the trees and make a kind of craft that would float upon the water, and then – for we knew already that the world was round – sail away in the direction that the birds had come from. Then, perhaps, we would meet up with others, changed as they might now be. Then, perhaps, there could be reconvergence, a great reunion, and we could begin a rich, new life here on Earth.

And some of this we did. Excited by such possibilities, Calvin worked feverishly, and many of his calculations now bore fruit. We sailed eastwards a long time, followed always by a sleek, silver form, the darker shape of her step-brother, and the larger, spouting outlines of her parents, grown now so much fatter in the freedom of the waves. And the rest, in one or another of its forms, you know: that we found a huge, green continent and, encouraged by that new fertility, began at last to breed; that there were mistakes; that the reconvergence never happened; that somehow, for all our trying, old enmities have continued, new ones have appeared; that Ralph, in his primitive frustration and jealousy, now rules maliciously in the seas, attacking, whenever Angelica is not there, any land-creature he discovers in the waves. Like all things tired of their pain, we have turned on our own deep longing, and although, like the birds, Angelica's family still calls to us in that ancient language of our tribe, for centuries, deaf and ignorant, we have slaughtered them for gain. Now, when dolphins stitch the waves offshore, as if trying to mend a seam that has come loose or find a causeway they have lost, although we search anxiously with them, I fear that the rift will not be mended, the bridge will never be found.

By day I walk the beaches, and sometimes I see her. By night I lie and listen to the sea rising within me, and know that I must drown soon. It is as if a different kind of rain is falling, a different kind of flood coming to pass, so much greater, so much more final than the last.

The White Angel of Mantria

I

There are some who oppose the substantivists, claiming instead
that their island and its legendary capital are incorporeal, of the
mind only. If it is to be perceived, they say, it is but in a certain
quality of the light in the paintings of Patinir, or, perhaps, in an
unlikely volume as a footnote that strikes its reader with the
clarity of ozone after the first drops of rain on dry ground. Their
Mantria is a sum of faint auras, emanations, a vast set of dreams
and predications arising from the disappointments of the
everyday. One of their strongest proponents bases his entire
case upon an inexpressible difference in the atmosphere of his
garden when walking out one late-summer evening just before
the last war.

True, this Mantria is made of fragile stuff, but the substantivists can offer little more. Over the centuries they have compiled
but a monumental chronicle of brief glimpses, of sightings so
momentary as always to leave their authors doubting that they
have seen anything at all. Indeed, although the guild of
Mantria's cartographers is a large one, there exists as yet no
clear agreement as to the size and location of the territory they
map. Many have returned from sea voyages with accounts of
majestic white-capped mountains seen rising above a distant
mist, of lush coastal jungles hedging the mouths of great rivers.
Some have even reported harbours, or what seemed to be
harbours, fringed with whitewashed buildings and towers so
roofed as to give the whole aspect a patina of silver. Yet always
there is an obscuring factor, some untimely aberration of the
weather or in the behaviour of the instruments, or some delay in

communication such as to prevent any verification of the existence or location of the sighting.

More bewildering yet are the accounts of those who profess with great conviction to have seen some fragment in their own locality. One, a painter with whom I have had dealings, claims to have seen down a sidestreet during an afternoon of rain a blur of a red quite unknown to his eyes, and which he can only describe as Mantrian. I too, when looking through a telescope atop a nearby mountain, once found my own city utterly and miraculously transformed, and yet, when I looked again, saw only the sordid and familiar prospect of my past experience. While I would hesitate to call this vision Mantrian, I can no longer assert with my old assurance that the island is a distant one – nor, indeed, that it is an island at all.

II

For as long as I can remember, my mind has been at the mercy of colour, not in its static or moribund forms, but as it shines from or vividly adorns those moving and vital about me. The rubies, let me say, that as a child I saw so often about my mother's neck as she prepared for a ball; it was never the stones themselves, but the way in which the light as it filtered through them seemed reflected in her lips or cheeks, or in the fire that burned so far within her eyes as she held me before her, a sun just waking far off across teeming water. And now my days revolve upon small focal points the colour of fresh snow: a shop-girl lays out watches before me on a velvet nap, her delicate fingers ivory-coloured against the black; the thick white hair of an old man rides like a small white wave upon pale eyes as he walks towards me in a crowd; I spend long hours of an afternoon listening to the tales of an old woman, a Madam who had known my city in the twenties and had, they say, the most beautiful girls in the country in her charge – and I but half listening, transfixed as I am by the white skin of her still exquisite wrists. I feel I am being summoned, and I long for a land where it often snows, where for months of each year the ground is covered with a thick beatitude of white.

III

I have become extremely sensitive of late to the tales of a friend whom I had hitherto dismissed as an incomprehensible visionary. Though spurned by most of Mantria's cartographers, he belonged, he told me, to an esoteric coterie, the members of which believe in a kind of Mantria *spezzato* – broken, existing only in its scattered parts. Ascetics, they think it a country won to only by stern mental regimen, by a careful training of the will and sight.

I have met them, and at last, it seems, I have an explanation of my strange enthralment, for this group has but recently discovered, in the library of a remote monastery said to have once been the retreat of certain captains of the Inquisition, an early and heretical discourse on the mechanical nature of perception, illuminated by Moorish figures and containing diagrams of remarkable insight and accuracy. Throughout, however, the author remains a sceptic, even unto himself, and the great bounty for my friends is to be found not in the treatise itself, but in a codicil in which this man discusses certain strange phenomena he there reveals to have been the source and wellspring of his doubt. He had himself, it seems, been subject to fleeting and fragmentary visions of a nature totally alien to his findings, and in pursuit of explanation had encountered, in works of his Moorish forebears, stories of an ancient city of the mind, a fortified mountain capital ringed by walls of different and symbolic colours – each somehow betokening a separate level of attainment – and topped by an earthly paradise within a palisade of silver. So like the Ecbatana of Herodotus, so like an untainted Babel, so Dantescan a climb has this seemed to us, and so keen our author's prose, that we have no doubt that we have found a fellow Mantrian.

But his theories of perception? His doubts? His brief, unaccountable visions? There comes, in his final pages, to my friends but a curious and enticing adjunct to their own researches, but to me with the force of a key long fervently desired, the story – no, the doctrine – of the Messengers.

35

And yet at first my hopes faltered. Each ring, each level of attainment in the gradual and universal construction of this city of the mind is prefaced, according to this man's account, by the appearance to the faithful – to the isolated workers, as we have been, in darkness – of an angel. An angel! All my hopes seemed dashed! For so many centuries since the founding and first corruption of that very religion which it had been my long desire to replace with a faith much closer to my own experience, men and women had seen 'angels', and the idea of angels had been given as placebo to the uncomprehending poor and desperate of spirit. Was I now being offered the same? Was this author at the last to prove, not a heretic, but a mere apologist for the very doctrines he had seemed, like me, to shun?

But no. Like the very Mantria of our coterie, these angels of our author are dispersed, diffracted by the dullness and confusion of our earthly life, having not the impossible and unacceptable wholeness with which the Church has so long presented them, but appearing as palpable and continual challenges to make them entire, to build for them a city in our minds.

And so I pursue the shop-girl with the ivory hands, the white wave of the old man's hair, the strange and beautiful face of an albino messenger; so I visit and revisit the ancient Madam as she reminisces of the milk-white skin of her girls, as she holds out for me her pale and still exquisite wrists, or pours a small, clear jet of water into her anisette, and so I stare for hours at the moon-white belly of my lover as she sleeps, the white angel of Mantria, my Mantria, dancing before me as in a broken mirror, leading me perhaps nowhere, perhaps – if I can but hold the vision – towards the first steps, or mid steps, or last steps of the city.

Du

Cities are remembered by symptoms of the minds that made them. The traveller enters them weary from the long descent from mountains, or unsteady from a rough sea voyage, or even, as he enters Du, sun-, wind-, and dust-burned, giddy in the sudden welter of scent and colour and cooling air. He does not realize that he becomes at once an instrument, first tuned and later played upon by the ancient makers of the place, the generations of builders, merchants and craftsmen who moulded its stones and have polished and worn them with the constant flow of their lives. Each cornice, should he stay so long, each step, lintel and well-curb will be found to contribute to an under-music, the eddies and ripples of which will be recalled, years later, as salve to the spirit's soreness, as counterpoint to some new measure in the time- and space-defying music of the mind, so that the present resounds, the past leans again into substance.

And yet the city of Du had seemed at first so different. I had been there many weeks, plying its streets and alleys, asking of the lives of its people questions which even now seem strange to me, before I began to understand why my past would not avail me – why, for all the beauty of such an oasis, the harmonies it awoke within me seemed so much to turn about a centre yet withheld. And still I do not know when first it was that its mysterious influence affected me, when first, blinded by exotic surfaces, I slipped unsuspecting into the undercurrent of that city and began my drift towards its secret centre, its still ineffable source. I can only say that, after an illness left too long neglected during months of desert travel, I arrived, and was almost a year recovering in Du. It was like a child's slow and gentle seduction into literature or music, beginning with a street-vendor's cry, a lullaby, and ending with Goethe, Bach, or Mozart.

One day I was sitting on a second-floor balcony overlooking the market with its dusty cornucopia of brass- and stone-ware, dried fruits and meats, livestock and withered vegetables, all now glimpsed and as rapidly obscured as the tide of arabs and westerners, africans and orientals washed over it. My coffee was strong and bitter, and the morning's heat enervating. As I sat I became intrigued, almost mesmerized by what it was that determined the placement of stalls, the flow of customers below me. One day, another day, I found myself far from where I was living, lost amongst streets into which only dogs and dusty pigeons would venture in the heat, and I realized that an urge unknown to the citizens had again driven me abroad, again marked the distance I had yet to travel to an understanding of this place. I was walking, another time, through the ungrassed, ungardened palm-groves by the wide canal when I realized that the old men who play chess in parks, cafés and piazzas the world over played here a game which, though no different to the casual eye, could be seen on closer inspection to be remarkably unlike. In each of these places my journey could have begun: in each, it now seems, it was already under way. In the City of the Game all things bear upon the stranger to the same effect, the dance of streets, the dance of customers, the dance of pieces on a board all linked, all governed by rules as deeply graven as topography itself.

In the old cathedral on the Beggar's Hill I found, in the tiled floor of the transept, a familiar pattern – or rather, beheld its possibility. In the Great Mosque, in a different part of the city, I saw, in the mosaics and the arrangement of the arches, its complement, its negative inversion. Day after day, as I walked the city or travelled in its ancient buses, I noticed the game increasingly, became more and more aware of its quiet popularity. People shrugged off my inquiries, joked as I observed to them its extraordinary hold: it was a game for older men, the city's self-advertising, a provincial embarrassment. Yet, in their own game in the streets, children hopped over fragments of its pattern. Yet the arrangement of cemeteries, the lay of so many private gardens, strongly conformed. Yet the city itself, when seen from certain angles from the hills outside it, faintly suggested, in its long boulevards, in the pattern of its blocks and parks, a strangely distorted playing-board, the domes and spires and battlements of its public buildings curiously like those of its major pieces, arranged in what positions of dance or conflict only the oldest and greatest masters of the game might guess.

I began to play. It was no easy task. While there were citizens enough of that place willing to tutor me once or twice in the simpler rules, the sub-culture of the devotees was so deeply bound into the city's life that all seemed to have a regular circle of serious opponents, a circle as unacknowledged as it was unbreakable, and which relied, as if by some unspoken pact, upon laconism and neglect to disenchant the newcomer. When I did find partners they were outsiders like myself, and no matter how much we played together there remained strange stalemates, inexplicable fluctuations in the board's terrain, to remind us of borders as yet uncrossed, of angles of vision as yet unattained. While our interest in our object did not wane, we grew tired of our repetitions and ourselves moved on, hoping that some new partner might have found some further fragment of the lore. I learnt in this way a great deal of the game, I learnt manifold purposes for almost every piece, I learnt to exploit somewhat its strange, asymmetric geometries, the cul-de-sacs its patterns could create, and my tenacity in pursuit of its principles made me, at last, something of a master amongst its outcasts, yet always there was within me the ironic certainty that the greater my acquaintance with the rules became, the keener would be my sense of my own ignorance.

There were, in this game, both black and white pieces. While I did not always win when I played them, my luck seemed tied to the latter, and I never won when playing the black. Although they would smile as if this observation but confirmed my naïvety, even some of the citizens, when I pressed them, admitted to a like affinity. Such, doubtless, is common to any game of skill or chance, yet in this city its hold, *where* it held, seemed absolute: those who discovered it in themselves became henceforward either Players of the White or Players of the Black, their abilities ruled by the colour, their judgements unsound when led by circumstance or curiosity to play from the other side. I was soon to learn that even for supposed scions of that city, such predetermination was by no means certain, and that many of those who had shut me out had not themselves discovered their colour, had been in their own way shut out by some deeper law of the game. Although the stirrings of my first interest in the game are now so hard to locate, it is quite clearly from this discovery of a mystic connection with its deeper roots that I date my true and secret initiation.

It marked at once a greater involvement and a distancing. The popular history of that city, I was to find, has it that once, at a time soon after its legendary founding, there had been rival factions engaged in long and bitter dispute, and that throughout the subsequent millennia those who have considered themselves its truest citizens have claimed descent from one or the other of these lines. Could it be, as some have claimed, that the modern game is a ritualization of the ancient conflict, a refinement of all its subsequent eruptions? Perhaps, although experience since has led me to believe that such legend, like so many others, is itself but a formulation of some deeper wisdom of the tribe. Always, it seems, and even in cities far from Du, there have been Players of the White. Always they have loved or befriended, conquered or succumbed to Players of the Black.

The game I found in Du was not, at last, the game I most sought explanations of. Although while there I never ceased to play, I became, within months of my beginning, at once dissatisfied with its intractable mysticism and ever more preoccupied by the differences between the boards which the populace now employed and those I saw on the floors and walls of the mosques, the churches, the old public buildings and palaces. Slowly, from these, and from what books I could consult in public and private libraries, I began, by rules and intuitions that the game itself had given me, to assemble something of its unwritten history. Although its beginnings, like those of the city itself, can only be matters of vaguest conjecture, I found isolable certain periods of the later history in which there seemed close correspondence between maps of the city, the interrelation of its principal families, and the manners in which the designers, builders and decorators of the time had incorporated elements of the game into their structures. Yet history did not simplify the questions that I took to it. I found myself tracing, not merely the variations of the board, but the lineage of its pieces, the evolution of their uses. I found the cities of the past, the cities *under* the city of Du, to offer not merely permutations of the game's topography, but positions, inter-relations that seemed formulae, encoded messages from an earlier time, what they said less important than that they existed to say, than the message behind their message, of a people intensely preoccupied with images of itself – a race who, throughout history, had so entered the life of its own messages that any separate identity was as impracticable as it was indefinable. The *gnosis*, the core of secrets that had so obsessed me as I walked the boulevards or haunted the palm-groves, began at last to seem a prison I might only narrowly escape.

My recovery by this time almost complete, I left Du by one of the desert-lined canals that join that city to the sea, and within weeks had returned to my former life. The freedom is not total. I could not leave the game so easily. It has become a part not only of the under-music of my mind, but of my understanding of the world about me. In this I do not know whether I am tainted or at last truly liberated. Sometimes my mind seems to rail at the bars of a cage; at other times that cage seems so large as to cast doubt as to whether it is a cage at all, and not, instead, of the order of things that define us. Several times since my return I have driven, late at night, up through the smog of my city into the mountains that surround it, where one can have a clear view of the stars. Always I can see in them configurations of the game. The code changes with the ages of the board and pieces I envision, and yet, it seems, the pieces and the board are always there, and always in pattern. Sometimes it is easy to think that I impose this pattern upon an otherwise orderless disposition in the meaningless dark. At other times I do not know whether it is my own mind or the sky that is the mirror – whether there is

not, perhaps, an eternal interchange of reflections, my own
mind shaping the sky which shapes my mind. Always I receive,
magnified a thousandfold, a feeling that I have down here daily,
that I am playing a strange, yet familiar role, my moves limited
yet still mysterious, my victories ambiguous, my partners
dominated by forces far beyond them, the ground shaped by the
constant flow of generations, and all around me the rambling
boulevards, the cryptic buildings, the markets and the palm-
groves and the obsessed, sad citizens of Du.

The Journal of Roberto de Castellán

The dogs and staring cats with which I now adorn the scene are products of my own imagination, though the birds and flies were real, as was the flesh they fed upon. The islands, too, exist, as surely as the human capacity for all that has happened amongst them. Magellan mentions them. Charles Darwin tried to land there.

They are called the Pergesas. I don't expect you to know them. Situated in the greatest of oceans, four hundred miles from their nearest neighbours, they are washed, as water sluices the bars of a drain, by a strong southward current that threatens all who set out to cross it with helpless dispatch to regions that in our time repel with their whiteness as effectively as once charts did with a dragon and the end of the world.

If they had a chartable history, the islands would have been called Purgia by the Romans, and have served as a hell for their exiles, but they are too remote for that. The Romans never got there. Instead it was the indomitable will-for-empire of Philip IV, well over three centuries ago, that saw the islands first accidentally populated by the human flotsam of a galleon-wreck, an odd and soon-confused assortment of aristocrats, sailors, churchmen, convicts and jittery warders from the colony of Puerta del Chasco, returning with beasts, birds and other specimens from the strangest of all the Americas.

Although would-be rescuers arrived at last, it was unintentionally and twenty years later. Both parties to this potentially momentous occasion decided, for reasons nowhere recorded, to decline the call of history, the ship departing swiftly and with no change to its complement. The islanders – for so, I suppose, we could call them now – did not remain so fortunate for long, however, and within half a century we find them annexed officially to the empire and used, as so many essentially worthless tokens of imperial expansion are, as a dump for criminals, a hiding-place for those the world would in any case rather not look for.

If, in terms of the human temper, the seventeenth century was very different from the one that preceded it, the eighteenth was even more so. By the time it had reached its tide-mark the population of the Pergesas had had leisure not only to nurture, from such unpromising seed, a small and more or less respectable community of farmers and plantationers, but, as if history itself were fashioned in concentric rings, to produce also a new, native and self-perpetuating complement of law-breakers.

The original castaways, that is, had had the good fortune to be thrown upon the first, largest and most fertile island of the chain. While not by any means of great dimensions, it is, unlike the others, large enough to boast a central range, run-off from which maintains impressively the rich volcanic loam of its foothills and the narrow coastal plain. Plantationers settled the richest lands, a host of poorer market gardeners the rest – until, that is, one was so fortunate as to discover in his plot a commodity somewhat more valuable than the humble cassava he had planted there. In harvesting this doubtful treasure, and in establishing a healthy trade, he cultivated also, in the manner of Cadmus before Thebes, that strange and ubiquitous variety of Sown Man known as bandit in such numbers that, when at last a round-up was conducted by an early governor, the island's rudimentary prison was quickly filled to overflowing. If less for humane than for political reasons – every burgher, it seems, had a brigand for a brother – the capital solution was ruled out and a gentler, yet at last more problematic one adopted. As the trouble was a product of geography, so geography was called upon to solve it.

Officially, there are seven islands in the Pergesas, although the figure must be regarded as arbitrary, the point at which an island becomes instead an atoll or a sand-encrusted reef being always, one suspects, a matter to be resolved between the mapmaker and his patience. A truly wise and conscientious man might add a dozen, perhaps a score, of hitherto uncharted islands to the group, showing it to be, as some have always known, not a chain but an archipelago, not a simple, linear progression, but a kind of coil, a minor swarm of submerged mountain-tips.

Of the seven officially recognized, only the largest island, Perga Mayor, has such notable fertility, that of the others descending roughly as their distance from this flagship grows. For this and other reasons they remained, until the round-up, almost completely uninhabited. Even then it was only Perga Menor – the next in size, the closest, and that which could most easily be watched – that was drawn into service as a natural prison. Upon conviction, felons, whether bandits or prostitutes, forgers or murderers, were ferried there, to take their part in what became a strange and rudimentary parody of the society that had expelled them. Male or female, aged or young, those who had committed crimes of sufficient number or severity were sent for a trial-by-wilderness, to be reformed or yet more thoroughly depraved as their Creator, the elements, or their fellow castaways determined.

As the decades passed and the century became more peaceful, the gaol on Perga Mayor, through an extension of its buildings and a gradual reduction in the rate of crime, was found more and more sufficient to that island's needs. Trips to Menor became less frequent, and even less was heard of its tiny and bizarre human ecology. Whether it was, as some suggested, a vicious and anarchic hell of unreformed, now almost-animal ex-criminals or, as others said, a struggling and near-harmonious community of redirected souls, no one then or now could truly know. Certainly the testimony of those few who managed to regain Mayor is contradictory, some claiming, before they were returned to their confinement, that they had escaped in terror from a predatory wilderness, and others that in that place they had, under the influence of like-minded folk, repented to the point where they could rejoin their families and friends. Trusting none, the government recorded very few, and forbade the island to the curious, threatening those that made unauthorized expedition with a longer stay than ever they intended.

What is known is that, some thirty-five years after the first unwilling settlement there, a boatload left from the far side of Menor in an attempt to reached the third island of the chain. Again reports conflict, depending, one suspects, upon the motives of the teller. Did they go because they had reformed, and wished to leave the terror of a lawless place? Or were they, like those first sent there, deportees of a society trying to cleanse itself? Were they themselves rejected by a law, or did they take law with them? If law it was that banished them, what resemblance did it bear to the other law, the law of the first banishers? Over ensuing decades there came further reports of departures from the prison island, but always these were shrouded in the same obscurities, and for at least a hundred years thereafter, uprisings, waves of crime, and political exigencies for which phases of law and order were supposedly expedient, demanded reactivation of Perga Mayor's unique cloaca often enough to prevent, it seems, any real contact with its populace until the middle of the last century, at about the time Darwin, had trumped-up quarantine regulations not prevented him, might have explored the archipelago's unusual ecology.

He would have found, had he but been allowed, a range of marine, bird and insect life to rival any he encountered in that strange and barren archipelago he was soon to make so famous. Cartago Bay never offered such an abundance of sea turtle, seal and dolphin. The shores of Indefatigable never displayed so rich and dense a mix of gannet, tern and frigate-bird, oyster-catcher and dotterel, nor, surely, so impassive an array of gull. Nowhere on Albermarle could he have seen such parrots, and even the range of finches would have vied, in its subtle adaptation from island to island, with that of Chatham and James. And if the Pergesas offered no black iguanas, no 'imps of darkness', they could have taught him at ground level, in their ubiquitous colonies of ants, spiders and beetles, lessons in the mutability of natural law that even the Galapagos did not give, each minute society adjusting with extraordinary ingenuity its rules to the demands of its environment, what had been inflexible law in one nest forgotten in another, where the ecology imposed different priorities and survival of the fittest bred what, a stone's throw away, would have seemed monsters.

It was not, in any case, until the 1880s, some fifty years after Darwin's passage, that any concerted attempt was made to yoke Perga Mayor's society with that of its unlikely counterpart, and then, some years after the last prison-boat had foundered, there was discovered on Menor only a small and primitive community of farmers and rock-fishermen whose morals seem not to have decayed as far as had their language, and who could convey with precision little concerning the society there of even a quarter of a century before. In huts at scattered points about the island's shores, hermits and beachcombers were also found, but their histories, like those of the villages, are lost, if ever they were properly recorded. Of those who had so long before left it from its farther side, the island, like its inhabitants, had no longer anything to say. It is to a very different source – the journal of Roberto de Castellán, a young officer employed in 1910 for a government survey – that one must look for what, if anything, is to be known of the castaways of castaways.

If, by all official accounts, the survey was a dull affair, yielding only minor adjustments to the charts, uncompromising soil samples and an unsatisfactory description of a wreck on a reef off the fifth island of the chain, the journal, left in store upon de Castellán's departure from Spain for Bogotá in 1916, suggests otherwise, and does so by narrating events of an ambiguity so radical that the young officer, his ship torpedoed in the Golfo de Cádiz, may be assumed to have died in their contemplation. De Castellán was not given to long journal entries: as he himself complains in several, his active and demanding employment left him little time for more than the most elliptical accounts. Even during his two years in the remote Pergesas, he would seem to have had little time or energy for writing. Yet of the four hundred and twenty pages covering the years 1909–11, the handful that describe his time in the outer islands are the most intriguing and show, more clearly than any others, a mind itself engaged in reading one of the darker pages of experience.

47

Of the days aboard the schooner, circumnavigating the islands or travelling between them, de Castellán does little but record the details of wind, weather and currents, and enter the particulars of specimens gathered in his capacity as *de facto* botanist, the naturalist who had been to accompany the expedition having at the last been certified too ill to do so – having been, in fact, too often too drunk to do anything of the kind.

Of the islands themselves, however, and of his days ashore, de Castellán's prose, while still elliptical, is more forthcoming. The isolation, the varying densities of foliage, the silences there recounted – counterpointed, as they are, by frequent signs of human habitation, whether fresh or long abandoned – nurture in the reader a sense of foreboding which, though de Castellán himself says little of it, they cannot have failed to create in him in even greater measure. This, at least, is the only way I can account for the passivity, the unsettling withholding of disgust, the strange moral lacunae that are, otherwise, too much like acceptance in his description of and failure to reflect upon the most horrid of the things that he encountered.

But to discuss de Castellán's response is to pre-empt the reader's own. Already I intrude too far. There comes a point in explorations of the Pergesas where diaries, the records of one's days alone must speak, and reference-points of tangible experience be allowed to rise like islands from our merer chronicles of wind and water:

Wednesday, February 2nd

Set out early in the dinghy with the Captain and Vincente, hoping that this side of the island would be easier, as it looked. We found a good channel through the reef and it was then only a short way to the head, on the other side of which there proved to be, as we had thought, wide sand before bush that did not look too thick. We beached easily and spent several hours in the vicinity. It was flat land and sometimes uncovered and so aided our tasks. Towards noon we found again signs of humans. This time cuts in two tall trees as if for climbing. I tried to climb but was not tall enough, and suspect that one must use a thong of rope or vine as natives do elsewhere. The cuts were old, but all the time after we had found them I felt as if someone were watching us. Captain Severino observed that shellfish had been recently taken from the rocks. As we left we thought we heard a playing, as of a horn or gong, and a kind of whistling, but then as we rounded the point there was the sound of porpoises, and it may have been that. This is the second sighting of human traces on this island now, and yet it, like all those west of Perga Menor, is supposedly uninhabited. The captain argues that any people that are here must be white, and cannot understand why they do not make contact.

This account was written of the third island, the one immediately west of Perga Menor. I cannot explain the 'supposedly uninhabited', unless it is that the men on the schooner had not heard of the minor exodus from the prison island so long before, or of the many since.

By the time of the next entry of significance the team had reached the fifth island, having found on the fourth – smaller and more exposed, with no high places and no fresh water – nothing of particular interest but a large colony of arctic terns. On the reef about the fifth, to which they gave the name Moret (having not yet heard of that man's resignation), they found the wreck of a vessel which they estimated to have been built in the early part of the last century.

Thursday, February 10th

This morning, although the sea had calmed somewhat, the wreck was still unreachable and we decided instead to row to the island. At the place where we could best beach the boat there are narrow strips of sand and rock platforms below crumbling cliffs. There are caves at the base of these which we explored, and before one of which we found human footprints which we thought fresh. Nearby we found a net made cleverly out of vines and large enough for two men to place across one of the channels. Vincente was carrying this back to the dinghy when a nearly naked woman rushed him from behind one of the larger rocks and beat him with her

49

fists, shouting sounds that seemed like Spanish words but were not as far as we could tell. We pulled her off Vincente with some difficulty and thought to tie her down but had nothing but the net to hold her, and as we tried this she broke free from us and ran back to the rocks. We looked for some time but could find her nowhere, and we think she must have escaped up the cliff. As we were unarmed we thought to go back to the schooner and to return tomorrow to look for her. Her skin was dark brown and deeply weathered and she looked to be an old woman, but as her strength and agility were so considerable we think she must be younger than she looks. Vincente says one leg and buttock were severely scarred as if she had been badly burned or lacerated, but neither Captain Severino nor I saw this. She had dark grey hair that was long and filthy.

The Captain, Vincente and de Castellán returned twice to the island, armed with rifles and rope, but while they found a rough path up the cliff and at the top a hut of branches, the site of several recent fires, and other signs of habitation, they could not find this woman or any other human. On the fourth day they sailed to the western side of the island and spent a further afternoon in search. Although again they found no sign of the woman, they did make one significant discovery. Lying in the long grass in a clearing overlooking the beach where they had landed, facing the bay and the island to which they next would move, they found a large cross that, upon closer inspection, proved to be the broken and weathered mast of a vessel, almost certainly that which they had seen wrecked on the reef on the island's eastern side. 'Tilted toward us on the slope,' writes de Castellán, 'with traces of its rigging rotting upon it, it but needed the remnants of a sail to resemble some great bird stricken there, halfway to the sky that waited at the top of the hill.'

While de Castellán muses in subsequent entries upon this, as upon the history of the woman they had seen, none of his hypotheses are particularly satisfactory, and all, in any case, are changed, if not in any clear way disproven, by his subsequent discoveries. The schooner left this island on Monday, February 14th. An entry of but two days later, while it ultimately may answer nothing, provides details so emphatic and so relevant in all their obscurity that beyond them, for most of us, there can be little to say.

'Relieved at least that those of whom we have seen the signs are or might be Christian', the survey party moved from Moret to the sixth and one of the largest of the chain. No reef hindered their approach. Having tacked to the south, they came at the island from that direction, losing sight of Moret behind the eastern arm of a wide bay. They moored there, but being near dusk they did not yet set foot on the island – again supposedly uninhabited, although by now they were taking no risks.

De Castellán's entry for February 16th reads as follows:

It is with difficulty that I constrain myself to relate the events of this day in their due order. At 10 a.m. I rowed across the bay with the Captain and Vincente. Having beached the dinghy near the south-eastern arm, we climbed its head so that we might first look over a wide area before deciding the day's activities. On attaining the summit, we could see all along the beaches in both directions – that facing south and that running northward and so facing Moret island directly. From the far end of this second beach, some distance back from the shore, we could see a thin trail of smoke rising, and we determined that it should be initially in this direction that we walked, there being besides some interesting commotion of sea-birds above the trees at a point almost halfway along. As we neared this spot, the birds for the time hidden by the high trees and dunes, a foul smell led us to think that they were wheeling about the carcass of some animal, though we knew of no very large ones native to these islands. Beyond the trees, however, we saw a sight much more terrible, for there was there a series of weathered gibbets, or gibbet-like structures, some seven in all. The first that we came to were bare, but on the others there were human skeletons, tied there strangely with fresh vines, and on the last, from which the stench came, and about which the sea-birds wheeled noisily, there were corpses that must not have been there many days. Although their eyes were plucked out, and much of the flesh about their faces and exposed parts gone, we could tell from their remaining clothes that they were the bodies of a man and a woman, tied to their places with vines around the wrist, neck and ankles, so that the middle parts draped forward most lewdly. Whether these people had been old or young we could not readily tell, nor stomach to discover. Nor, although their horror seemed to fascinate us strangely, could we bear that place for long, and soon retreated, calculating that whoever were many enough to kill or so suspend this couple were too many and too dangerous for us. Captain Severino remarked, as we walked back along the beach, how strange it was that such a thing should seem to stare so directly across the strait at the place where we had found the mast but days before.

And after this there is almost nothing. The men returned to the schooner and de Castellán records that they spent two days circumnavigating the island, as close as possible to the shore, watching for further signs, and surveying twice more with their binoculars this horrid sight. Doubtless they spent far longer discussing what they had seen, and how much of it they should reveal.

Bad weather at last prevented them from returning to the island, just as, according to their official Report, it did their intended passage across open sea to the most distant and most isolated of the chain. But here, in the official account as in de Castellán's own, we come across perplexing disparities and hiatuses. While failure to reach this last island – Gómez, as it is now called – seems a likely development of weather forecasts in de Castellán's entries of February 18th and 19th, it can, in fact, be neither confirmed nor denied by reference to the journal, which for no apparent reason breaks off here, to be resumed as arbitrarily in late March with accounts of de Castellán's search on Perga Mayor for an early berth to Buenos Aires. Yet surely there is some disparity between the fact of the schooner's arrival at Perga Mayor on March 10th and details given in the Report concerning the failure to sail on to Gómez. From the island of the gibbets to Perga Mayor is a voyage of little more than ten days – let us say twelve, if we are to allow for bad weather. And yet the schooner – beginning its return journey, according to the Report, on or about February 19th – took almost three weeks. The journal, of course, tells us nothing of this intervening period, and the Report is not scrupulous concerning dates. Between eight and ten days are missing – time enough to search the fifth or sixth island more thoroughly; time enough, perhaps, to have visited Gómez and to have learned what, if anything, was to be learned there.

Strangely enough, it is, of all these things, to that, and only that, the seventh island of the chain, that de Castellán refers in later volumes of his journal, and then but as the subject of cryptic references – jokes, perhaps – that I cannot claim to understand, likening, at one point, the sea about it to a mirror, and, at another, the 'Beagle' to a diamond that was cutting it in half. And then, in what we must assume to be de Castellán's penultimate volume – that which covers the first eighteen months of the Great War – there comes, as he contemplates taking ship again, and so faces the prospect of the Kaiser's Absolute Blockade, an enigmatic reference to his personal situation as 'this seventh island'.

Whether by design or some perplexing aphasia there is, moreover, as little of the gibbets in these subsequent volumes as there is in the severely edited Report. One might almost argue, were it not for their grim inconclusiveness, that such things were Roberto de Castellán's fiction. I do not think that they were, nor do I think that that can ultimately matter. De Castellán himself died in a barbarous war of which his country had no clear part. It was an absurdity, an irrelevance, the result of an unexpected collision of incompatible laws that was itself indication enough that we need neither maps nor history to encounter whiteness, dragons, the edge of the world. As if, ultimately, the map of the world *is* that of the human soul. As if that soul were stretched, as at last it had to be, on the rack of its own wilfulness, torn by the very things that serve it.

Blue

It was a summer of fires and shark attacks. No rain for four months. Every day the newspapers brought accounts of foreign wars and preternatural disasters: a planeload of people disappearing over the Bay of Bengal, a volcano in Indonesia, floods ravaging central China. The fish were not biting. All around The Head, for all the dry weather, a strange blue mould grew on people's cheeses, a new and unknown species of mushroom grew from rotten timber and the damp earth under water-tanks, and all that could be caught in the Bay were a few blue-spotted, brown, grouper-like fish at first rumoured to be poisonous, though many ate them without ill effect.

The rain itself was never properly reported. The editor and staff of the local paper were away at a weekend conference in the capital, and, although the evidence was everywhere, all of us were somehow impressed into relative silence by the majesty of the event. And who, anyway, would have believed it? When asked later what led to their strange preparations, those who would talk at all spoke of a recurring sensation in the nose and sinuses as if of the ozone after rain, or of a feeling under the tongue as of that left by a bursting cardamom. This reply, while true enough, was usually sufficient to deflect an idle curiosity, though in truth it was the dreams that started us. Not prophetic dreams exactly, and none of us could really say how we got from them the sense that all our floors and our belongings should be bared. One dreamed that he was bathing in an open cage, the swallows darting around him as he scrubbed. Another dreamed of crossing a high, wooden balcony with her lover, and seeing at the other end two women standing in mannequin postures, looking out to sea, their pale green dresses ragged and

54

their long hair bleached in the sun. Another, my brother, dreamed of receiving a long-awaited letter, and taking it to a huge bay window. He smoothed out the great, blank page at the table and tears came to his eyes as he read it, again and again with rapture.

How so many could have interpreted such diverse things in so similar a way I cannot tell. Perhaps the sight or rumour of what others were doing influenced their understandings; perhaps there were dimensions to these signs and portents that none could detect or consciously register. Whatever it was, in Vincentia, in St Mary's, in Albatross and Mooney Creek and all the small hamlets in between, on hillsides, on neighbouring streets, on curves of the highway, roofs came off the houses, the panellings of weatherboard and fibro left the walls, and here a man could be seen showering in a cage of two-by-fours, there a family could be seen in their lounge-room watching the sky over their television, in the manse at Albatross the housekeeper could be seen through the gaps in the bookshelf she was cleaning, staring across to where the SP bookie was tearing the paper from his shop-front, digging away at the putty of the windows, and from the first stirrings of this strange exposure, just after six on Friday, to the time of the shower on Sunday evening, people all down The Head began living out-of-doors in the comfort of their own carpeted rooms, sitting up late by unseasonal hearth-fires, making toast as they had once done as children while all the stars of the southern hemisphere attended. True enough, we laughed at ourselves, but we sat there just the same, rugged against the cool night air, listening to the possums, yarning as we hadn't since our honeymoons.

And at last it came by the bucketful. A short, torrential pour which none could have predicted and which all, mysteriously, recognized as the only true and likely culmination of those strange three days of air and light. Children ran about with buckets, the young people danced, and we who are older just sat in a mute amazement: a short, sharp burst of blue carnations, tiny blooms like great, sky-petalled snowflakes in the evening dust. And we knew, all of a sudden, how terribly, terribly thirsty we had been, and we sat there or sang in the phenomenal rain, and something deep within us was drinking, every stem, every petal, every tiny, perfect flower, slaking, in that long, imperfect summer, a deep, deep need for miracles, for something a little more than rain.

The Lost Wedding

Miss Jennifer Cooley lives amidst tall trees on the edge of town with a dog that hoards things under the house and a cat that stays mainly on the roof, where it stalks sparrows. In her rather sequestered existence in between, Miss Cooley is hardly ever seen but for the one morning a fortnight when she does her shopping, and for one week each year when she does a kind of spring cleaning, during which time she sometimes hangs upon the line out back a faded wedding dress in the style of twenty years ago.

They say that every town and village has its crazy person. I wouldn't know, and I'm sure Miss Cooley isn't, but certainly she is different. I think people call her crazy because they need someone like that, and since she keeps to her house so much, and when she does come out has such a lost look about her, she fits most readily into the role, whatever better candidates there are. It's mainly the young, anyway, who call her mad; older people have a sort of respect for her.

You couldn't say her behaviour is all that strange. You don't see enough of it. And her circumstances aren't really all that different from others in the town. It's her story that singles her out – so strange and so well known that it's become something of a local myth.

The church she claimed it was all going to happen in is a little convict-built chapel half-way between Albatross and Vincentia. On the day it's supposed to have taken place she had got almost there – close enough to see, from the top of the hill, people milling around the door, just beginning to file in, someone who looked like her uncle standing in the lych-gate, and the sounds of the old, windy organ cranking up to play 'O Perfect Love' –

when she had to turn back, having forgotten something which is now forgotten, or at least uncertain, but which must have been somehow vital at the time, a piece of old jewellery, or the bridal bouquet, or something else that you get superstitious about on occasions like that. And when she got back there was nobody there. She went right to the door, thinking that they would be waiting inside, but the place was locked, and there was nothing, only the dusty road, and the hot sun beating down, the cicadas, the long grass stirring faintly over the graves.

When at last she dared to mention it – she was too embarrassed, of course, at first – nobody knew anything about it. They were rather surprised to hear that she'd been thinking of getting married at all. Indeed, some – even some she thought she'd seen at the church – were perturbed that they'd not got an invitation. It was as if the whole thing had been an illusion, a mirage, a figment of her own imagination. And yet she distinctly remembered it all – the groom (though he hotly denied it), the proposal (beside the hibiscus outside the Albatross Town Hall, on a hot night near Christmas), the preparations, the congregation around the church door.

It might, people said, have been that she dreamt it. The world of dreams and the waking world are often so similar that, moving from one to the other, we can be quite unaware that we've crossed a border, and everyone has a story about one time or another when they had thought they had done something they'd only dreamed they'd done, or that they knew someone they'd only dreamed they knew. But it's hard to dream something that takes a month or so, proposal to almost-happening, let alone to remember it all in such detail, and for a long while Jennifer Cooley thought instead that she'd been the victim of a conspiracy, a cruel practical joke. At last, however, she conceded that too many were involved for that, and everyone remained so adamant that nothing of the kind had ever happened that she decided, eventually, that she must simply have lost it, in the same, exasperating, incomprehensible way that one can lose other, more tangible things – a gold watch, say, or a pair of spectacles, or the clipping from the *South*

Coast Record, that shows one with the biggest silver bream ever caught in Mooney Creek.

A few years ago, my father mentioned one night that, when he was much younger and she more beautiful, he used to dream about Jennifer Cooley. And on the wharf once, shortly before he died, I got Old Man Cooley to propose the astonishing hypothesis that something very like what had happened to his daughter must have happened to his father's sister. Generally, however, when I mention the lost wedding I get the feeling from the older people that it's not a thing to talk about. Nobody, anyway, seems to have much to add, though sometimes they look as if they might. It might be that this business has been around so long that some are not as positive as they used to be, and begin to suspect that somehow, somewhere, they too might have lost it. After all, a wedding must have a congregation, even a lost wedding. It seems to me that there must be a whole lot of lost things around, just under the surface, if only you knew what they were, or where to look for them.

When she talks about her wedding, as she sometimes still does, Jennifer Cooley keeps changing things – one time, say, it'll be a brooch she goes back for, another time a ribbon – as if fitting the wedding into the real history of things were a bit like a jigsaw puzzle, or like one of those shapes that in the children's game you have to get into the right-shaped holes. Maybe she just doesn't have the right shape yet. Maybe there's just one little, niggly thing that stops it all from slipping neatly into place: perhaps it was grevillea, not hibiscus, outside the Albatross Town Hall; perhaps it had not been 'O Perfect Love', but 'Love Divine, All Loves Excelling'; perhaps, if she had spoken up earlier, if she hadn't been so nervous, someone might have remembered, and this silence, this blankness, this awful process of forgetting might not have set in.

John Gilbert's Dog

William Hovell, John Septimus Roe, Paul Edmund ('The Count') de Strzelecki, Louis de Torres, Charles Throsby, John Claus Voss, de Freycinet, Cristóvão de Mendonça, Nicholas Kostas, Wommai, Lieutenant Tobias Furneaux: almost exclusively, the real history of my country has been the history of its exploration. The names of its discoverers, fêted in the court of Portugal, or lost in the Great Sandy Desert, echoed in the schools of my childhood and were taken home as projects to be researched in the encyclopaedia or, more actively, in a series of explorations long before begun in the furthest corners of the yard and soon extended to daring, morning-long ascents of the mountain that began at the end of the street. Even now, what I most remember from my early summers are the days of discovery, afternoons when the heat in the houses would drive us out to picnics in Westbourne Woods or the Cotter Reserve, or down to Lennox Crossing, now so many fathoms beneath the surface of a man-made lake. In the one it was the world of endless pine-trunks, the thick carpet of dry needles that could be scraped into ships or fortresses; in the others it was the vast forest of bullrushes with the beaten, trodden places that we made our camps, or the world of the rocks and water, the thick ti-trees that, on nights at Scout camps years later, would fill with real torches, real staves, real raiding-parties.

Later, in school holidays, it would be the dunes of Huskisson. Alone or with others, I would press further and further down the three-mile beach towards Vincentia before turning abruptly inward, grabbing for clump-grass, pulling myself up through sliding sand towards the moment when the reliable familiarity of the ocean side gave way to the unpredictable. One day it was to find dense and impenetrable scrub, another a stagnant lagoon, another the yard of a delapidated shack, another, to my great confusion, only the back fence and chook-pen of our summer landlady. Now, decades later, when I sit down to what I sometimes think of as realer matters, each paragraph, each set of images that might begin a poem or a story, can become a track through bullrushes, a path through ti-tree, a sliding climb through clump-grass that might lead, yes, into the street I am living on, but also, as it sometimes does, into a place I had never imagined – as if one were to climb into the familiar ash tree in one's own backyard, only to find that it now continued, that its boughs joined other boughs, its leafy arcades others, until there were systems, treescapes, countries that had been inconceivable before.

One kind of exploration ends, another – if the myths, the traditions, the childhoods are strong – begins. Of history, as of the parched, dust-covered men on exhausted horses, a linear progression ceases and the lateral, the vertical take over. The lines on the charts, once straight and simple, begin to turn back on themselves, to buckle and convolute as more and more is known, until the maps resemble less a primitive rock painting than the surface of a brain.

II

In one of the drawings of a Dutch artist whose work I have long admired, files of human figures are moving in opposite directions on a staircase. If we follow either line – the one going up, or the one going down – we find that, although the figures never reverse direction, and although the stairway continues to rise in front of the one set and descend before the other, the head of each line meets its tail, the four turns in the stairway having formed a square in which, although there is a strictly limited number of steps, there is one flight perpetually rising, another forever going down. Both flights are the same flight. We call this an Optical Illusion, which is our way of denying that somewhere this place, this same set of stairs, exists.

This denial, this shutting of the gates, is perhaps just as well, for if it were possible that this staircase existed in space, it would have – since all ascents and descents take some period to accomplish – to exist in time also. It would then be possible that, just as the figures perpetually climb or descend, yet perpetually meet the tail of their own line, so time passes and yet never advances, and that, as it both advances and fails to advance – as it moves forward only to repeat itself – so there is alongside it a time scale that perpetually 'regresses', perpetually repeats itself, another temporal zone, moving in a direction opposite to our own.

In Canada, working on a thesis through the steaming summer, I would turn from a dull passage in some academic text, and look out from my second-storey window, and there would be the leaves of the chestnut, with the tunnels along the branches, the secret passages. Then, as sometimes even now, I would imagine myself entering, penetrating even further than before. And what if, now, today, I should do that, should go down one of the corridors, follow it through all the turnings and the bough-lanes? Would I find myself, my earlier self, the young child in his ash world, or the student in a hot Toronto summer? Would he know me? Would he understand me? Would I believe what he had to say?

Is this inconceivable? I don't think so, for surely human life itself is so to any other creature, its extravagance and its wonder so great that few of us ever get out, or wish to, from under its perplexing shadow, but instead spend all our days numb to its true dimensions, so afraid of the hugeness, the strangeness revealed by every wayward step, that we have long ceased to take such steps and in preference pass the time until our end in the drawing of closer barriers, the erection of walls, as if each new word were a wolf, each strange thought or angle of perception a barbarian on a thunderous horse, bearing down upon us, his spear already launched.

No. Nothing is inconceivable. Life itself is so unlikely that our very presence denies the privilege of denial. If our time is a thing that moves 'forward', if 'distance' is a thing that separates, if 'reality' is distinguishable from 'dream', if human consciousness is, as I sometimes suspect, a flickering circle of light about a dark, bewildered centre, these are only our terms, our language, the small salvage of the bewildered from the incomprehensible, and may, as yet, be like the myths that supposed primitives have evolved to explain their universe: that the moon is an ancient hag chasing her wayward son, that the stars are the sand flung up to blind her. And who is to say that the very extravagance of the human imagination, pedestrian as it might seem to a greater eye, is not another 'reality' beckoning, as a child lures a pony with sugar, or a dog is thrown scraps from a table? An explorer's dog – John Gilbert's, say, or Watkin Tench's – gnawing at the shin-bone of a beast he's never seen before.

III

This early evening there is a cool breeze through the coral trees. I can detect the faint, almost imperceptible scent of the jacaranda that at the end of the yard is coating the gravel with its lilac blooms, and from behind me there comes the drier earthen smell of potatoes baking. I am sipping hot tea and thinking of the beauty of objects in this cool grey light that has in it the first faint touch of darkness. It is the artist's light, the light of still life. From my balcony every shade of the leaves' green is discrete and the trees are wholly at home in their bodies, as if they, too, need the first hint of death in their senses to live truly. In my small flat, with my busyness, my debts, I would call this moment one of luxury, my balcony in its green cathedral, the smell of the potatoes baking, the birds beginning to sing – three different sounds already – and every object distinct.

A man is whistling as he zig-zags up the stairs of the building opposite, and an Indian woman in a red top and bright orange sari pauses on the landing to call to someone I cannot see. She is a splash of rich colour through the leaves. Moments like these – so particular, and yet almost without identity – seem as if suspended between worlds. One could be nowhere but here, and yet here could be anywhere: in Australia, in Brazil, in

California, in India. The woman standing on the stair is unaware that she is poised upon a border, that she has just stepped very nearly out of time and place, that this moment, as she goes as usual to buy milk at Constantino's, she has stepped into composition, that she has entered a page, a frame, and is at once devoid of identity and, in a sense, more full of her identity than she has ever been.

Black

For several weeks now my world has been cancerous. Not a normal rebellion of bodily cells, but an insidious revolution of the light. It began one morning, after a long night at my work-desk poring over a problem in St Augustine. The night receded improperly. Or rather, if no less *properly* than ever before, to a vision that had utterly changed.

I had watched the night withdrawing many times, charting always with joy or wonder the manifold incursions of the dawn, its rays breaking first as a pale penumbra over the low, black mountains, becoming soon a thin crust of light, then gradually informing the bare plain before my window, the mulga, the fences, the still-dreaming horses, the wheel-less, rusting har-vester slowly rising as if from a deep river, from black to dark grey, from dark grey to milky indigo-blue, from indigo-blue, as the first warmth swallowed the last wisps of mist, to the greens, browns, olives and ochres of the day. But that morning it was different. The rising sun, the galah-breast of dawn, and all the surfacing colours and objects were there, but it was night's residues and not the rays of light which absorbed me – the flat, horse-shaped things that spread out from the hoofs of the mare and foal, that shrank slowly into them, to be almost completely swallowed by midday, reduced to a small, torpedo-shaped slash of darkness on the grass; the tall, cross-hatched dark that lay beside the fences, that the fences drew into themselves (that *retreated* into them!) as the morning progressed. All things, it seemed, soaked up their portion of shadow as they took on their corporeality, as if, to *be* in the full light of noon, they must first contain their allotment of night. I began to nurture a growing conviction that one of the primal forces of life – its sixth element – was for the first time being revealed to me, and that the insight of Grosseteste, the great wisdom of Scotus Erigena, should at last be inverted, should now proclaim that *everything that is, is dark.*

I found, as I wrote, that words – black cracks, black rivers – revealed the true darkness of pages. I found it lurking under every stone. I saw it scuttle into corners when I opened the doors of the barn. I saw it deep within they eyes of horses. In wonder I went to the mirror to find it staring at me, to find it, as I grieved at the awful porosity of skin, even in the whorls of my fingers. All that day – that day, and many thereafter – I sat out in the yard under the great, dark leaves of the fig, watching its ripe fruit welling with purple, knowing the darkness within things, nursing my own, longing – as does, eventually, the terminal patient, for whom death becomes at last an intimate knowledge, a profound validation – for the 'night' to come, when the dark could seep, and trickle, and gush forth, could fountain and fill up the fields and houses, and all things could give up their blackness, the earth rebelling against the tyranny of light.

And now I belong to another place. Everything I write is dark. All my words and actions have shadows. I perform, I work amongst the heavy ghosts of daytime, yet know that with every handle, every creature I touch, I am stroking an inner night – that in the clock-face, in the continual rotation of the hours, there is the perpetual battle in which I am a defector, an apostate, riddled with doubt, not knowing, when I say *is* or *seems*, if I say *dark* or *light*.

The Misbehaviour of Things

All day outside my bedroom leaves have been falling. This in itself is usual for this time of year, and does not disturb me. It is one leaf, just one – not the first to fall, but nearly the first, and not because it has fallen, or because it has not, but because, in a way, it has done neither.

Outside my window this morning, after the alarm had rung, I saw it depart from its branch. The break was clear. One had no reason to suspect abnormality. But then, after the first few inches, it stopped, or nearly stopped: there was, at least, a marked deceleration, as if it had changed its mind or the laws of gravity had been somehow suspended. Instead of increasing as it drops, the rate of its fall has diminished as the day has worn on, so that now I begin to doubt whether it will reach the ground at all – so that now, when I say, as I just did, that all day outside my bedroom leaves have been falling, the statement contains another quite different one, that all day one leaf has fallen, in a most extraordinary way.

Over and again throughout the day I have returned to it, but nothing has changed. Each time I look through the window I can see it has dropped further, but always a little less further than before. Everything else in the garden seems normal – or did this morning when I went out to look. Now, with all else that has happened, I'm not so sure that I would risk it.

I have been used, for a long time now, to a certain unpredictable malfunction in the things around me, days when my car cuts out in mid traffic or when pens refuse to operate at crucial moments, when a knife or razor cuts one despite all reasonable care, or a sheet of paper slices one's finger. The failure of a toilet to function properly, for example, can be a shameful admonition, and a car that, parked outside while a man visits his lover, releases its brake or spontaneously starts, leaping a gutter and breaking through a neighbour's fence, can seem a most vindictive thing. But, for all that I am wont, at such times, to refer to the Malice of Inanimate Objects, this is often but tripping, but stubbing one's toe against the Real, and the true causes, if I could trace them, would as likely prove to be within me as without. Such events have their purpose. Warding off complacency, guarding thus against larger neglects that might otherwise prove disastrous, they assist in a kind of balancing, and have about them a periodicity that is almost predictable. But what has been happening today – what has, I fear, only just begun to happen – is something more sinister, an abdication, an unmistakable Misbehaviour of Things.

It is not all things, mind you. Just one or two. But the number is gradually mounting. In a way, I admit, it may not be so much wilful misbehaviour as a carelessness, a lack of attention. A thing is not where I think it is – or rather, *is* there, but is also in a strange way not. I see it and it acts as if I don't, as if it isn't, or as if, somehow, *I* am not – at least, not in the way I am used to.

One mirror, one only, of all the seven in the house will not reflect me. I passed through its room with a cup in my hand, and had, as I approached the far door, the unsettling feeling that something there had not been normal. It took me some moments to discover what was wrong, but soon I realized that, whenever I passed the wide, reflective surface above the sideboard, the vivid green of the lawn that it reflected – the white garden furniture, the grey paling fence – remained undisturbed, refused to acknowledge that I had walked between them. At first I thought that this was an optical illusion, some freak blind-spot in my own retina or in the arrangement of the light, but this had never happened before and the mirror's failure persisted even when I pressed my face against it. I checked my reflection in several others, and all attested my corporeal existence: the abnormality, it appears, is not in *me*, but in the thing itself.

Temporarily reassured, I spent the morning in other tasks, trying to resist like an incipient neurosis the temptation to revisit the sideboard and the bedroom window. I prepared and ate a leisurely lunch, as it was Sunday, and encountered no problem. The fillet was as rare as I intended; the salad behaved; I could see my reflection in the knife-blade, the white rim of the china plate. Everything, that is, proceeded normally until the wine-glass. With this, however, within a very few minutes, I found myself engaged in the strangest and least explicable tussle of the day, a misbehaviour – if that is what it is – more subtle, more complex than the rest.

As is my custom, in moods of particular indulgence (perhaps this time it was consolation), I had opened a wine of my favourite variety and region, though of a year and vineyard I'd not tried before. On such occasions I prefer to drink after, rather than during my meal, so that the flavour of the wine can come to me uninterrupted, and stay with me into the afternoon. My meal finished and cleaned away, I sat again at the table, poured myself a glass, and, having for a few moments savoured its colour and bouquet, lifted it to my lips, to experience what can only be described as an abrupt hiatus, an inexplicable absence only vaguely approximated by saying that no taste occurred, that no wine entered my mouth. The phenomenon was momentary but there followed a set of astonishing transforma-tions. I lifted the wine again, and it – the fluid – seemed to stay where it had been, a few inches above the table, shaped as if still contained within the glass. Attempting again, I managed at last to taste it, and, relieved that for once it seemed to behave, took more than a sip, yet when I replaced it on the table the level in the glass had not diminished. Intrigued, I went to lift the glass a further time, only to find that, while it appeared to be there, surrounding its parcel of dark red liquid, my fingers encoun-tered only the glass-shaped wine, and returned to me wet and shiny, as if they had squeezed the grape itself. Now, wanting a draught, I did not know which part to place my hand upon, which thing – the fluid or the glass – might next give way, hoping that it might be the fluid, wondering, when at last the glass and fluid came again together to my lips, and again I tasted the rich oaky nectar, that they could at the same time remain untouched, the light on the delicate meniscus unbroken by the slightest ripple of my presence.

Sometimes I wish that, instead of the tales of romance or intrigue that appear so constantly on the new book stands, I would find a Book of Ordinary Things and Gestures, that could show us how extraordinary they really are. There is a part of me that is dying to rush out and catch the leaf and thrust it to the ground. There is a part of me that wants to go to my nearest neighbours with the wine-glass and beg them to witness its misbehaviour. But somehow, now, there is also a part that knows that, if I were to do these things, nothing would be received, nothing would advance at all, and a gap that is here already would become only wider. And how do I know, anyway, that it is not me, breaking out of my body, bigger and stranger than I ever thought I was?

The Line

Late, on the hottest night of the year, he sits by the window. For a long time he searches for a line and at last he finds it, beginning at the tip of his pen and continuing across the page beneath the words *continuing across the page beneath* until it reaches the edge and, independent of ink and human motion, and pausing only briefly as if about to dive, moving thence on to the desk and past the candle and the glass towards the sill.

From there, against the first faint stirrings of a cool breeze from the river, it slips through the wire screen and out across the fuchsias and the lawn. Traversing the pavement, rising above the trees, and following no streets or feasible cross-country route, it passes westward over Roe Street and the Beggar's Lane to the playing-fields and the old stone buildings of the university. Not stopping at these, nor in the café quarter, and following roughly the course of the river, it passes through the wide updraught of denser oxygen above the park, directly above the last bedless lovers in an E. J. Holden and the pointing arm of the statue of Sir John F., the founding father of the city, and thence across the long, perfect reflection of the Great Port Bridge and into the sleeping suburbs. After almost one mile of these, just grazing the upper branches of an avenue of flowering gums, it slows and descends, approaching cautiously the third front window of a darkened house four miles or three pages of the city directory from where first it left the orderly confines of the introductory paragraph of a tale for which it may, in truth, have never been intended.

To follow it by car (public transport, needless to say, is unthinkable), one would have – to employ again the city directory – to begin on page 48, in the square designated by the fine blue lines that descend from either side of the letter *B*, and those which stretch towards the left from the number 53 at the far right-hand margin. Bearing in mind that one's general direction must always be westward, one would then move at first in a southerly direction along Alton Road until Balcott and, turning right at the church with the great rose window, move diagonally across two map squares to where the page joins 47 and, crossing at first Charles Road, Balcott leads into Dean Parade. Now moving directly westward, one traces Dean through four squares of the light blue grid – past the city pool, the council offices and the Ladies' College – and passes beneath the freeway into Estuary Road, where the Floral Beach Parade and map 46 begin. Following the Floral Beach Parade diagonally across the upper right, beside Dog Swamp and the Herdsman Cemetery, one finds oneself, having strayed north-westerly, referred to map 36, where the Floral intersects Green Street and turns towards the sea. At Herbert Street one takes a left-hand turn. Moving again southward, one drives beneath flowering gums to a lane beginning, of course, with the letter *I*, and halts at the darkened frontage of number 38, at a considerable disadvantage and at least half an hour behind the line which, unshackled by a pedestrian imagination, has already entered the third window from the left – left open to catch the cool sea breeze – and passed between billowing curtains towards a bed upon which sleeps a woman with soft white skin and auburn hair, her face partly hidden by her furled right arm and a fold of the single sheet. Uninhibited by this last barrier, the line has long since found her, and, not without an initial parabolic digression, proceeded along her left calf and thigh and come to rest, peacefully and without thought of return.

She, of course, knows nothing of this. She has, in fact, been borrowed from Alain Dufort,* and was last seen on a balcony above a courtyard lined with palms. All she could tell is that, when she awoke, she had been dreaming of an old man on an esplanade, feeding seagulls that, for their own mysterious reasons, suddenly rose, and, banking westward, traced with their soft grey wings an ambiguous message, free of grid or narrative, on a dark sky promising rain.

---

* *Font de nuit* (Paris: Hibbert et Fils, 1914), p. 27

The Poet N.

In the years since my exile ended, since the government changed and I became able, in my chosen city, to continue in relative comfort my search for something like a mastery of my native tongue, I have seen much of the poet N. Although I cannot claim in any clear and confident way that he has aided me – although his erratic behaviour, his lying, his chronic unreliability have caused me no end of embarrassment – I have clung to his companionship with a tenacity that has continually amused my friends, and the reasons for which I have only recently begun to understand. It is something to do with his fascinating alchemizing of the simplest words; something in his insidious inversions of the language which, once comprehended, cries out, like a reef, for record.

Last year, at the height of the long, dry summer, I spent five days in a beach-house to which N. had retreated with his family, unwilling to pay the high city rents of the tourist season. It was there, one sultry afternoon of brooding cloud, listening to him digress in his incipient drunkenness on the work of an obscure eighteenth-century writer, that I caught at last, like a flash of the lightning we had all been waiting for, that vital connection between the man and his work – between the chaos and the beauty – that until then had been only a nagging evanescence. For an instant, clearly and unforgettably, I saw the link between three things which had strangely beset me: N.'s wonderful, yet somehow profoundly disturbing poetry, his habits, let's say, of mendacity, and, somewhere behind these, the regime which had exiled me, which had taken the lives of so many, and which N. had yet miraculously survived, despite rebellious behaviour, despite his dictum, loudly proclaimed, that in this world one lives not by the rules, but by the ways in which one breaks them.

The link is language: the way he changes and subverts it; the way in which, in conversations with him, something one has used as a metaphor, an image, an illustration, can become *reified*, turned into a *thing*; the way in which an innocent word can become, in his discourse, a counter in a nefarious attempt to shrink and to contain the world through a set of secretive descriptions of its principal ideas and phenomena.

Already I describe it badly, but I am struggling, after years of enthralment, to release myself by chipping away at the chains which seem to have bound me: they are made of words, and I have only words to serve me.

It is true, of course, that the attempt to weave a net of words around the world is one we are all engaged in, but in N.'s hands, while astonishingly poetic, it has become, since it begins every day anew, a particularly limited and repetitive process, never able to get very far from its ground or to develop a convincing and coherent system through which the world might be the better understood. It fails, indeed, to become much more than a set of small and fragile monuments in a vast desert, around which eddy, like hot, dry winds, too many things that are not grasped, not understood. And surely it is not insignificant that these small and temporary marker-stones that his conversation erects, and around which it so formlessly flows, are rarely if ever the true products of his own imagination, but are collected by him as a bower-bird collects the materials of its nest. As they talk of poetry, of art, of sex or geography, visitors to whatever house N. lives in – he is remarkably nomadic – leave fragments there unwittingly. They find, if they stay long enough, words or images they have introduced used subsequently in contexts they had never dreamed of, and to which their offerings seem singularly unsuited. It is as if they had brought their language to a Hall of Mirrors, a hall of no ordinary kind, but of the distorting reflections of a Fool's Gallery, a circus sideshow. Expecting to speak and to be spoken to intelligibly, they find, not Articulate Man, but his nightmare, not the teacher, but the pupil's parody, a charlatan, a naïve and unconscious iconoclast, who though he seems to pursue their arguments with an earnest good faith, constructs instead their negative, their desolate inversion.

Looking for explanation, we find ourselves faced always with the same confusion: denied a formal education by his impoverished childhood, his notorious years in prisons and reform homes, is it that he has turned against the more fortunate in a jealous and bitter satire, or is it instead that, observing for so long the methodologies of those thus envied, he is in fact their earnest mimic, a disadvantaged autodidact, convinced that at last he does as others do? Even now I cannot tell whether, in his heart of hearts, he loathes or envies me. Even now I do not know whether this man – this genius – is comic or tragic.

And yet his works are there, rising over and again from confusion to a statement so strident that it seems to taunt us with our indecision. Not quite monumental, perhaps, they none the less present us with a remarkable breccia, a conglomerate studded with lines of astonishing force. If only rarely are these lines worked into cohesive wholes – if only sometimes can we see their function in a wider symphony – they yet appear like strange and hard-beaked Birds of Paradise, swooping over our shoulder as we struggle through. They are bright, beautiful stones picked up from a gibber plain, or actors, dressed in the finery of illustrious figures who, though they haunt us with their familiarity, are ultimately unidentifiable, and walk before us playless, speechless, companionless on an empty stage. Forcing us to try, because the entire weight of our culture has trained us so, to piece together these stones, to write the play of these characters – forcing us to look, in parody, in irony, or in a deeper, mystic application, for some cohesive explanation of his apparent contradictions, his elusive usages (a task which might test our own ingenuity more than it does his work) – it may be that he helps us to answer one of the most significant questions of art, of how it is that poets, novelists, painters can create so often works and characters that seem wiser and deeper than themselves.

And what is it, after all, but the beauty of an occasional pebble, the epigrammatic force of a line about loneliness or death – our own obsessive conviction that beauty and truth, beauty and vital order, must be somehow connected – that leads us into this maze, this wild goose-chase, this search for coherence? Is N., perhaps, a proof to us that they are not so nearly tied? In our own dogged attempts to alter, to resolve, to *mis*read his poems, are we trying to reclaim our language or to retard it? Do we find, in the rebellious work of N., that phenomenon which so many philosophers and aestheticians have so long sought, the art that is no longer the mirror of the human mind? Do we stare, when we look into his finest works, at some sort of natural wonder, like the wind-carved cliffs of St D., the gorges of the River M.? Or do we look instead into the products of a Mind and Process that we cannot yet comprehend? Is this work poetry, or only the place where it starts?

It was, indeed, along these lines that my own thoughts ran before the lightning flashed, before somehow I was given the boldness – the temerity – to see instead the playroom of an infant such as those once called *terribles*, the *poètes* they called *maudits*. And then to turn my back. Too many skeletons implore from the shadows. Whatever else lies latent in the mind and works of N., I cannot but see that we find there, in a particularly condensed and dramatic form, the secret history of our vicious century, of words wrenched from their things, of language that, employed as costume for our masquerade, has lost its innocence; that the bright pebbles, the crumbling cairns of N.'s windswept desert, have the names of our ancestors, our families, our own lost selves upon them.

Depth of Field

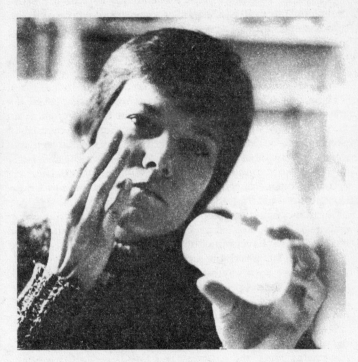

When the camera lens is focused to give a sharp image of a particular object, other objects closer or farther away do not appear equally sharp. The decline of sharpness is gradual and there is a zone extending in front of and behind the focused distance where the blur is too small to be noticeable and can be accepted as sharp. This zone is known as the depth of field of the lens. It is often miscalled the depth of focus.

The Focal Encyclopedia of Photography

I

Jazz alters the night. I have placed some on my turntable for that purpose. Perhaps you will do the same. It suits much of this story, although later a strange silence might intrude and eventually dominate. For the moment the music, a floating horn and a gentle, undulating piano above a softly brushed cymbal, transforms this dull, box-shaped room on the first floor behind the jacarandas into a high-rise apartment, the lights of the flats next door becoming, through the open weave of the curtains, those of the harbour in a greater city on the other side of the continent where he, the character supplanting me, has moved to take up a new position.

He knows nobody well there, and for a week now has spent his days becoming acquainted with the city and his evenings unpacking what has been left to him after his recent divorce, the principal reason for his relocation. The apartment, as yet, is relatively bare: boxes of books, clothes, kitchenware and miscellaneous artefacts fill the second bedroom, and etchings, a woodcut and some photographs in aluminium frames lean against the walls in the living-room where there is at present only an armchair, a circular table, and a swivel-chair intended for a desk. It has been oiled recently and too well, and already a few dark drops have stained the light grey carpet.

It is all, in fact, much the same as here: one need not go very far from one's own life to find a fork in the road, a door into another hall. Jazz plays on his record-player. He sits at the table and smokes, looking out over the harbour to where the ferries radiate from a central terminus or return from their harbour-suburb destinations as if tracing the blades of an invisible fan, or the fingers of a giant hand. They carve the black water between the small islands, the warships and freighters with Greek or Japanese or Italian names, and the wounds they make gape momentarily and whitely behind them. Before him on the table, beside his wine-glass, is a small pile of papers he has found in a drawer in the wardrobe, evidence of the person, male or female, who occupied the apartment before him: brochures describing the sights of Los Angeles and British Columbia, some dog-eared blank envelopes, a book of matches from a Lebanese restaurant, a photograph, a sheet of paper with pencilled directions and a map to what appears to be a place off a highway west of the city.

It is the photograph which holds him; the head and shoulders of a slim woman with dark eyes that stare straight at the camera. They disarm him. Although obviously it is the photographer that the woman knows, and not this man who looks at her image some unknown time later, there is, in her eyes, an apparent knowledge of the person she is looking at, a familiarity that, once recorded, is there in some strange and haunting way for all who look at her – as he looks at her now, inheriting an emotion not intended for him. Not that that emotion can be easily identified. The woman is neither smiling nor truly frowning, though there is, perhaps, a hint of displeasure in the eyebrows, the clear downturn of the mouth. If anything, she is quizzical, as if the photographer has just said or done something at which she does not know whether to take pleasure or offence.

The jazz has stopped. I am experiencing a moment of that silence I told you about. Outside I can hear the coral trees and jacaranda rustle in a light breeze off the river. It must be similarly silent in his apartment. He looks at the photograph a while longer, then pushes it away from him and rises, turning out the light. With the room in darkness he can see the harbour more clearly. A ferry is moving towards the wharf at the foot of his street. He can see the white wound of the water behind it, as if the craft as it moved were unzipping the surface of the bay and forces of darkness were rushing to restore it, smoothing rapidly the places where the ferry had exposed the strange white flesh.

He drinks the last of the wine and then goes to the bedroom, undressing slowly in the moonlight from the window and lying for some time on his back, staring into the grainy dark before turning on his side and attempting sleep. As he sinks towards unconsciousness she moves through his mind like a prospective tenant in an empty house, or like a tenant leaving, checking for last things.

II

In this place he has been sleeping long hours, waking tired and disturbed from vivid dreams, uncanny distortions of the world he has come from. This morning it is different. The dream he leaves is of a city he does not recognize. He is on a crowded cobbled street, between Tudor houses, and he is riding a bicycle, weaving precariously through the steady flow of pedestrians, trying to find a particular number, the address of the woman in the photograph. Half-way down its length the street is divided by a main thoroughfare and is, by consequence, numbered separately along its eastern and western arms. At the appropriate number of the eastern end he finds only a deserted apartment-block, its foyer open to the street and cluttered with building materials, spars of light outlined sharply in the dust-filled air. Running, abandoning his bicycle, afraid that he will wake before he finds her, he makes for the western end of the street through a crowd which has thickened dramatically. He reaches the number, pauses for a moment, then places his hand on the bell. It is the bell of his alarm-clock. He turns it off and gropes back towards the doorway, trying to find her, to have her answer. To do this he must retrace his steps, and the whole dream falls apart, tears like tissue in a wind.

Dreams, too, create false familiarities. He thinks about the woman as he showers, dresses, prepares breakfast. While he drinks his coffee he sits for a few minutes with the photograph. Her hair is short and even, as if newly cut. It looks dark. He notices that there are pinholes in the corners, in the white border around the picture, as if someone had fastened it to a wall, as if someone else had stared at it a long time.

III

He returns at ten, after a dinner at which he had drunk little, listened a great deal to new colleagues. For two hours he sorts books and browses the newspapers. Just after midnight, still too alert for sleep, he pours a glass of wine, turns on the radio, and sits again with the photograph.

She is applying cream to her face from a small jar. He looks at the hands. They are thin, bony, and large-pored like her face, but not delicate. The fourth finger of the right hand is slightly crooked as if it has been broken, or warped by some kind of repetitive work. The lines between the phalanges are deeply grooved, and the knuckles stand out, as do more strongly the metacarpals as she holds out her fingers to touch her cheek lightly. The hand is a fine combination of delicacy and strength; an artist's, a craftswoman's. It looks raw, as if it had just been washed, as if she had been handling paint or clay. The other hand, closer to the camera, holds the jar delicately between the tips of fingers and thumb, and the palm – which, below the jar, is held towards him as if for reading – seems also raw and, distorted by the perspective, disproportionately fleshy. It is slightly out of focus; the lines are illegible. He looks closely for some further sign of her occupation. Although it is only her face that is in sharp focus – her face, and the wrist of her sleeve – there seem to be crude shelves in the background, with dark, squat objects upon them. A studio? Something in the light, too, suggests it: the background bleak, washed out, as if under fluorescent lights, although here the light comes from her right, just above the level of her shoulders, and its source may in fact be a window. At what time of year? Her clothing suggests winter, although the light seems too strong for that.

IV

There is another dream, more intense, more difficult. This time he has found her. They are at a restaurant, familiar, friends. The place has booths of an old and heavy wood, rough-hewn, and tables of a similar make. All is bathed in a dim, honeyed light. At some point in the meal his wife joins them and – although the three share a bottle of rich Carpathian wine and sit with their heads bent forward, almost touching, as if conspiring together – he and the woman find themselves frustrated by her presence,

81

unable to touch or speak as they wish. He is aware throughout of an astonishing charge in the air between them. When at last some friends call his wife away the woman leans into him, whispers, touches him. He can feel her arm and the side of her breast, and can smell her hair. It is a moment of deep and extraordinary physical communication, and is like the healing of a wound. When he wakes he is aroused, tense and confused, and must stand for more than twenty minutes in the shower, slowly reinheriting the world. It is a week since he first found the photograph. Something disturbing is happening. It is not love. It is something other than that.

V

He shows the photograph to a technician in the laboratory, an amateur photographer. She explains to him the principles of depth of field, and how the depth of focus in a photograph – the width of its stable ground – can be used to determine something of the lighting conditions under which it was taken. This picture, she points out, has a very narrow depth of field, its sharpness extending only from the girl's wrist to her lips. The jar is too close to the camera to be within the field; the eyes are slightly beyond it. This indicates that the shutter of the lens must have been wide open, to take maximum advantage of the light. This light, moreover, must have been very weak, for his friend points out that the grain of the photograph – the way that the emulsion on the surface of the film has so evidently formed itself into the tiny particles that, blackened by the light, have formed the image of the woman – shows the film used to have been a 'fast' one, produced to allow the use of a fast shutter-speed in low-light situations. Even though such a film has been used, she notes, and despite the wide aperture of the shutter, the tips of the fingers of the right hand are slightly blurred, indicating that in a further attempt to compensate for the weakness of the light the shutter speed had been set too low to quite freeze the action. The photograph was taken at dusk, or – for as a *coup de grâce* the technician turns over the photograph and notes that it is printed on paper available only in the United States – in the weak light of a winter's day in North America. To whom would one send such a photograph? Who would bring it so far? The woman's expression reveals a sadness, a darkness that one would want only one's intimates to see: a dear friend, a lover, a sister. It does not say *I am happy*. It says, if anything, *I do not understand you. Where do you come from? I wonder who you really are?*

VI

The third time he dreams of her is very different from the others. It is early morning. They are walking through a ruined city. Although the sun is rising through a thick smoke-pall, the air is very cold. Against a foreground of jagged masonry and half-demolished tenements, the sky is dramatic, angry, as if the fire which has just swept the earth is contiguous with the heavens. They move along a street he once lived in. She points out the houses of his friends, the shop where he used to buy groceries. They are all in ruins, and there are people working in the rubble. He recognizes some of them and waves. At the corner they light cigarettes from a red packet. There are distant sirens and there is much activity, though immediately around them it is very quiet and still. As she shields his match from the wind he sees that her thin hands are white with the cold, and that she is shivering.

He dreams this early and wakes in darkness. Realizing that he will not sleep again for a time, he lights a cigarette and gets the photograph from the next room.

VII

The eyes are a camera. You can see, if you look very closely, that they are not totally black, as they might at first appear, but that the pupils are greatly dilated, as was the shutter's aperture at the time of the photograph, wide enough to make best use of available light. The depth of field narrowed accordingly. It is as if my lover's depth of field has also suddenly narrowed, and I, as I angle myself for a better perspective, am moving out of her area of focus. Her eyes are the eyes of departure. I knew, the moment I saw them through the range-finder, that she would not come with me, that she could not leave North America, that the question I was about to ask was an impossible and aggressive one that could lead only to our mutual embarrassment and pain.

Of course, there are other photographs. In some of them she is smiling, in some she is talking animatedly, and in one she is sitting, deep in concentration, over the clay on her wheel. I have kept most of them. It is only that one that haunts me, only that one that I could not bear to take with me a second time, but left in the drawer, hoping that she might lie quietly, that she might stop her strange fighting back, her strange, infectious demanding of what, after all, has been denied to both of us.

VIII

The needle clicks unnoticed at the end of the record. He has pushed the photograph from him and is sitting with his elbows on the table, his fists over his eyes. Beyond the balcony the ferries ply the black water, trailing the tiny comets of their wake as if the dark were seamless and the harbour floating in a sea continuous with that of the stars. The ferries all have the names of noble women, governors' wives: *Lady Edeline*, *Lady Street*, *Lady McKell*.

I do not know if he is weeping. Somewhere, in a confusion of messages, he feels that he has lost some further part of himself, and does not know what has brought this upon him. Although the eyes of my lover now seem as dark as the harbour – although that is why he has pushed her away – he does not blame them; he does not think that they have anything to do with it. And perhaps not, although one can find easily enough accounts of primitive peoples who get angry at those who photograph them, believing that with each image they lose some part of their soul.

The soul becoming angry at its loss, its expression – its wrench – fixed for ever in the image, transmitting for ever the message of its violation, the soul of the photographer becoming increasingly attenuated across his images, etc.

IX

He comes to a dark, swiftly flowing river, the water clear but with the black tinge that comes from peat-marshes. At the shore, on large boulders, there are old women, squatting, washing articles of white linen, beating them on the stones. Over the river, pale and almost luminescent in the grainy light, a man is standing by the mouth of a cave, naked and looking towards him.

He, too, is naked, and the stains from the clothes of his body are already fading, rinsing out in the stream. The women are singing. The water is very cold. Its strange, translucent darkness breaks into white furrows around his knees, his thighs, his belly. Soon he is swimming, against the current; long, powerful strokes towards his body.

Striptease

Striptease is another of the codes, a fringe, a border. I would know no more about it than I did at eighteen, were it not for Mia, and at eighteen all I knew was Tony Capo's version – and, of course, what I had seen for myself, on weekends when we hitched to the city more or less for that purpose. At that time it was more of an escape, a vent for frustration, than love or an interest in the semiotics of oppression. Neither of us had ever had much luck in talking girls to bed, and when at last luck came the wild nights in the city ceased.

They had never been very wild in any case. For Tony – for both of us – the world of striptease, then, was an Aladdin's Cave. There could never have been more than a handful of nightclubs in S. (it was not a large city), but for him there was always another as yet unvisited, a better, newer one where the girls were more beautiful, more daring. Sometimes, it's true, we found them, but almost always, after an unrewarding show or a long, vain hunt through back streets, there was disappointment, anger, embarrassment at finding ourselves yet again victims of what seemed uncontrollable urges within us.

With Mia it was all quite different. By then it was nine years later and I was living in L. The provincial capital of my earlier explorations now seemed truly provincial. I had been married and divorced (the girl who, in my third year of university, had put an end to Capo). I wrote during the day and gave evening lectures. My child was being raised elsewhere.

An hour each midnight, for a week before I met her, Mia had been sitting at the rear of the Soho, where actor friends struggled nightly through a set of improvisations. I had been going there for some time, after lectures, to talk with the owner–manager. On the night I met Mia the show ran late. In the dark, trying to disturb no one, I had taken the seat beside her.

I knew early that she was a painter. It was weeks before she told me that she was also, when she needed the money, an exotic dancer, an artist of the striptease. I don't think such news would ever have made much difference, and by that time, in any case, I was in love with her, or had admitted to myself the possibility: love is always to some extent an act of the will, a conscious decision.

This is not to say that, as our relationship intensified, there were not late-night cross-examinations, even brutalities. Striptease, I found, is a labyrinth, a maze within a vast house of mazes, a puzzle of emotions, as much as of social relations. As before in my life, with other people and on other subjects, our late-night introspections eventually became giddy and bewildering descents into deeper and deeper levels of our motivation, to the point where any conclusions seemed only exhaustions of the will or vision, and any attempts on my part to dissuade Mia from dancing or to demonstrate her complicitous position served only to reveal my own ambiguities, my own complicity.

But this is not a story about Mia. Nor is it really a story about striptease. It goes *through* them, like the weak spot in a floor, like the first clue to something larger.

In certain scales of our measurement, neither comparison of an 'above' and a 'below' nor of the territory on either side of a frontier will give us an idea of essential structure, for each side reflects too closely the other, is too much dependent upon it. It is only at the shores, the borders, that we find free space, observational territory. Striptease is a border, a fringe. I have called it a code, but I am not really so sure. To speak of a code is to imply that something, some message, has been put into a different language – perhaps fabricated, perhaps even gibberish – in order that it appears to be other than what it is, and that those intermediaries before whose eyes it must pass will not understand what it is that they see. It implies an ultimate recipient who understands. It implies, also, an encoder, a transmitter with a desire to deceive. And who, in this case, are the intermediaries, who the transmitter?

For two years, on and off, I visited clubs in the city. Sometimes, pursuing interests or acquaintances formed while in Mia's company, I went without her. Most often, however, my visits concerned her directly, whether to keep her company when she performed in some unknown quarter, or simply to watch her dance, and perhaps to comment upon variations to her act.

This, however much its details changed, followed always the three-song format standard at that time. Whether these were played on a juke-box or by a live band, whether they were current hits or old favourites, whether their lyrics had any reference to the act itself or were instead quite irrelevant, depended largely upon the nature of the audience, the place of striptease in the club's routine, and the personality of the dancer – her attitude, and perhaps that of the management, towards her act and audience. Sometimes the choice of song was arbitrary, but as often as not it was a key-signature, establishing for actor and audience alike a tone of irony, aggression, antipathy, seduction.

During the first of these songs the dancer would appear in full costume – sometimes that of a fantasy (a lion-tamer, a schoolgirl, a many-veiled concubine), sometimes something very like street clothes – and would strut or dance as sensuously as possible about the area allotted her. An article of clothing might be removed – a cloak, a veil – but at this stage little was ever truly exposed. To entice the audience, she might simply bare her legs, or allow, in her dipping and turning, a glimpse of the skimpier coverings beneath her outer layers.

It was during the second song that most of these were removed. Almost always, at the end of it, the dancer stood in sequined bikini alone, in the third song doffing her bra to reveal her breasts, and often the lower portion to show, beneath its small triangles, that even smaller arrangement known as the g-string.

Timing is important. It is as bad for one's act to become naked too soon as it is to remain dressed too long. The second song – the transition – is crucial. More than mere rehearsal, the art of striptease requires a sense of proportion, of structure, of the rhythm of the whole.

There was, of course, within this strict framework, an accepted variety of execution. Just as in their costume the dancers might vary from the exotic to the girl-on-the-street, so in their movements, their modes of display, they ranged from the modest to the disconcertingly explicit. When city regulations allowed, a good manager would ensure, if the show was continuous or ran in sets of dancers, that every third or fourth would be more daring, more forthcoming than the rest. Now the girl would undress more swiftly or have far less to wear, and much of the third song would be given to more provocative behaviour, often a period of slow contortion on the floor in clear imitation of the sexual act. Although, in effect, the striptease here had ended and a performance of a different order had begun, a vestige of the original remained in the manner in which, deliberately or otherwise, the g-string was allowed to loosen and sometimes slip aside, affording some of the audience glimpses that the management might not have intended.

Dancers whose acts were of this kind often worked harder and were paid more, not merely for their greater exposure, but because such gymnastics as they employed could require skills and a suppleness far beyond those required of other dancers. These, some would say, were the true exotics. More daring, perhaps more erotic, they were also a vanguard of a sort, for their presence or absence on the circuit and the reserve or extremity of their acts reflected week by week the fluctuating tolerance of their society.

Underworld murders, a wave of sex crimes, a council election, a public official's need to restore credibility – these and many larger factors could have significant and often immediate effects on the striptease, forbidding in one month what was widespread in another, the world of the dancers expanding and contracting with the greater systole and diastole of the city. From their vantage – one hesitates to say 'as if from below' – one saw the campaigns of religious groups, the reactions of provincial or national authorities, the automatic responses of the various policing forces less as social improvements than as surface activity in a bizarre but stable moral

economy, a kind of cosmetic with which the aged organism of
the city retouched itself, prepared itself for its own dances, its
own striptease.

In Poland, in the first months of German occupation, pornography became available as never before. Some say that it was
officially sanctioned in the hope that it might reduce resistance
not only by promoting the isolation of one individual from
another through the substitution of relations of fact by those of
fantasy, but also by generating, where real relations occurred,
selfish, aggressive and manipulative attitudes complementary
and receptive to those of the Reich itself. It might, of course, also
be argued that the presence of so much pornography was a
symptom of, or response to, isolation and demoralization that
already existed.

The instance is extreme, and, in any case, the relation of
striptease to pornography is ambiguous. Certainly striptease
has served a like purpose even for the most benevolent of
governments: certainly, in providing the small reliefs that it
does, it distracts or reduces the demand for larger. But it is not
clear that this is sufficient reason to seek its prohibition. Indeed,
one might ask whether attempts to restrict or eliminate
striptease, futile as I suspect they must always be, do not
involve their proponents in a greater hypocrisy – do not, in
attacking a symptom rather than a root cause, a mirror rather
than the thing reflected, threaten one of the means by which
society might see itself the more clearly.

In its promises, its enticements, its feints and withdrawals,
striptease is a rite-of-possession and of denial-of-possession. As
much because it parodies as because it rehearses, it has become
an essential part of a society which, to survive, must drive its
members from purchase to purchase, consumption to consumption – a society which must, by the unflagging creation of new
and 'essential' luxuries, dispossess as it gives, placing always, as
the dancer must deny always the dream she keeps alive, an
invisible barrier between the consumer and fulfilment of desire.
Perhaps this is why striptease seems to bear a constant,
ambiguous relation to the economic life of its society. It is as if

the society must always display, somewhere about its person, its secret – as if striptease were its honesty, its obscure confession.

Mia *chose* to dance, to arouse, to become naked in public. The atmosphere, the hours, the exercise and attention all contributed. She was aware that to some extent she was both a victim and an accomplice in what it is customary to call the degradation of women, but, she said, it was a victimization, a complicity, a degradation she could *see*. I watched her many times as she undressed before strangers. Always it was and was not Mia. The face and body were hers – the high cheekbones, the dark helmet of hair, the taut belly with its thin silver scar – but they were worn like a mask, a sign that floated only at the surface and behind which meanings changed, drifted, compounded to a depth I found incalculable. To undress, to expose, to dance and accept tributes, to show so evidently that she existed behind and above these things, she argued, placed her beyond those who watched her, beyond the system in which she took part.

Yet in all this – in my accounts of Mia, of the city, of different parts of the code – I seem to lose something, to ignore some vital element. I find myself pursuing it through the prose as if it were some final revelation, an ultimate gift or discovery such as those that the dancers offer. I had thought to say that I was writing about sadness, about desire, but there are so many ways to approach them, and it is, at last, something other than these.

At the Golden Palace, as I remember it, the dancers perform in a kind of wrestling ring on a platform above the seated audience and open to it on three sides. Tables are placed flush against the stage, and others extend off into the darkness of the large mirror-walled room. On the fourth and enclosed side of the platform are a partition, behind which the dancers dress, and large speakers which thrust out music selected by a disc-jockey who sits in an elevated booth on the far side of the club. The striptease is virtually continuous from six to well past midnight, and as the club is downtown there is a considerable office and tourist trade. The audiences are enthusiastic and are kept so by bare-breasted waitresses who circulate constantly with full drink trays.

The dancers here are amongst the most beautiful and talented in the city, and are encouraged to be the most daring by the number and size of the notes that members of the audience fold and hang on the ropes about the ring. In most cases this offering is an attempt by a spectator to bribe the dancer into paying particular attention to his sector of the audience – to bend or display herself in his direction, to show him something she has not shown others – but in some it is a simple homage, and the bill-hanger retires into the back of the hall with no attempt to catch the dancer's attention.

It is a busy and violent place. Even when it is less than half full the lights about the stage, the flashing mirror-balls, the volume and rhythm of the music make it seem crowded, excited, enthusiastic. All, at the Palace, is pace, lights, movement, expectation.

The Star Lounge is a different place. Once, perhaps, the doyen of such venues in the city, it had subsided, by the time I knew it, into a genial shabbiness. The carpets, as I recall them, are still thick, the brass of its older fittings still gleams, but rows of formica-topped tables have taken over the dining area, and the periphery of the room is discretely shaded as much to hide the wallpaper as the transactions that take place there. Shows are at nine and ten thirty. There are always two or three dancers. Sometimes there is also a singer or comedian. Like the waiters, the barman, the organ-percussion duo who bracket every set with a few bars of 'Satin Doll', the stocky transvestite (once a truck driver) who compères has been there for years.

If it is at clubs like the Palace that I have seen the most daring and explicit of dancers, it is at clubs like the Star that I have seen the most naked, for there it is that one finds the youngest and the oldest of performers; there it is that I have seen them dance with punctured arms, with bruises upon their bodies like flesh flowers, and have felt I was not so much watching as learning to read. Everything at the Star Lounge is slower. If it becomes, as a consequence, somehow sadder, it is also more erotic, perhaps even more artistic, because the darkness is allowed in.

There is, of course, a circuit in the city, or rather a set of interlocking circuits, that dancers ply throughout the year. Seldom will they stay at the one place for more than a week, though they might return to it a few months later. As they age or their acts lose currency, they slip from the orbit of the more glamorous clubs and find themselves in second or third billing at the Star, as often as not on the same programme as others whose fortunes are rising. This constant movement within the system reflects a similar movement of the system itself, is itself a circuit within a wider circuit. The Golden Palace always exists, though it may change its name, location and personnel. The Star, more stable, may not change its name, but from month to month can seem a different place. Watching these clubs as they are closed down or forced to shift from one part of the city to another, reading the cryptic communiqués on their padlocked doors, one begins to realize that, in this as in many other aspects of society, disappearance does not mean that something has ceased to exist, but merely that one has lost sight of it. Striptease is quicksilver. Once, in an attempt to ensure that no unveiling extended beyond the G-string, the city passed a by-law that all dancers must wear at least one item of clothing at all times. At the Golden Palace dancers first completely removed their upper clothing, then, replacing the bra or halter-top, removed completely their lower. Focusing, as they were thus led to do, all their attention exclusively on one and then another part of the body, their acts became more explicit. (The Parrot, situated as it was on the farthest street of the borough, simply moved across the road.)

I dream, sometimes, that I am in a huge, dark house. It has not been occupied for years, and is in an advanced state of disrepair. I think I am trying to find something. I do not know what it is. As I walk carefully around an upper storey in the moonlight, aided by a dim torch, a part of the floor collapses and I find myself amongst fallen masonry and a rain of dust on the bare boards of the floor below. As I begin to explore this a similar thing happens and I fall again. The process repeats itself and I keep falling. The house seems to continue indefinitely. The rooms I fall into vary in size, so that at times I drop only a short distance, at others a long way through huge, empty halls. In some cases the floor's collapse is almost immediate; in others I am able to explore the room at length. Eventually all these rooms come to seem so familiar that I begin to wonder whether I am falling in a circle. I still do not know what it is that I look for, unless it is that weak spot in the floor, where the solidity of the room gives way and my fall through the huge, dark house continues.

In another dream I find myself again beside Mia. We have just had an argument and she has turned away from me, weeping. I'm crying too but I don't want her to see it. We've said cruel things to one another. They seem to have come out of nowhere. Soon we will begin a long, exhausting search for their origins. It is as if we are each afraid that we have shown too much of ourselves, and are angry, vulnerable, trying to retreat. Timing is important. It is as bad to become naked too soon as it is to stay clothed too long.

The solitude of the striptease dancer can be extreme. Up on a stage or behind a rope cordon, before a dark audience, taking her own clothes off, her entire performance is ghosted by the usual privacy of such an act. As she disrobes and turns her nakedness in the light before us, showing, with her perfections, her scars and her bruises, she exhibits openly that vulnerability which most strive to disguise. What is normally hidden or reserved for those one loves is taken to strangers. Presented without apparent shame or fear, it becomes thus a challenge, a threat, as much as a submission or a supplication.

Of course, we think, she is paid to do so, she is a kind of prostitute, but in large part this can be true only so long as she thinks of herself so, and few dancers do. It might be argued that the need to classify her thus is a need of the system which created her and which can accommodate what she reveals only by extending to it its own materialistic criteria. To put a price on this nakedness is to suggest that there is some necessary connection between the existence of such vulnerability and the money that is exchanged for its exposure, as if these were products and not stubborn human facts – as if the bruises, the scars, would not exist if they were not paid for.

In my country, times of widespread social protest – times when the public has tried to force its government to recognize the social danger, the human risk of its policies – have also been times of widespread public nakedness, unpaid-for, unasked.

Baubo, to comfort the mourning Demeter for the loss of her child, lay down and, pulling her shift above her waist, raised her legs and held them wide apart to reveal a child within. In like manner, if for different purposes, the Sheela-na-Nog of Celtic legend exposes herself, grabbing her labia in both hands and thrusting her open vagina into the face of evil. There was a time when her huge sex, like that of an African fetish, adorned church walls or jutted from cottage lintels, fending off invisible intrusions. I cannot help but feel that in some way her relegation in our society registers the force of an evil within it. Faced with the mourning of Demeter, faced with all manner of intimate invasions of our hearth stones, our holy places, what shall *we* do?

Roses

At her house – they lived in separate places, though by now spent almost every night together – he sat outside by the barbeque, watching the fire he had made. The sea breeze had arrived and was stirring the branches of the eucalypts in the corner of the yard. Some evenings cockatoos would come to them, black or sulphur-crested, or grey and pink galahs. Tonight in the sky there was nothing but a few high clouds changing their colour slowly as the sun set and the blue twilight deepened. Already the stars were out and a huge moon was visible, low and full over the house next door, accentuating the stark lines of its iron roof, the outline of the lemon trees that huddled beside it.

Some time that morning, in a room three thousand miles away, his divorce had been finalized. It may have been while he was breakfasting on the balcony of his flat downtown; it may have been as he drove Kate to work; it may even have been, given the time difference, before they woke. He did not remember thinking about it much until, leaving work early, he called in to the station bookshop for a book he wanted. He had bought three. One, a collection of letters, lay on the table, a surprise for Kate when she came outside.

Something had happened. She had been delighted by the book. She had leafed through it while they ate, and even read him some passages, but then she talked about her husband. He'd heard it before, this obsessive working-over of old facts and arguments, trying to determine what had gone wrong, trying to salvage, to apportion blame. He'd done it himself. It was a necessary process, but as it continued you got further from the truth, not closer to it. Soon the memories became vague and incomplete. You began to suspect that you were fabricating. By then, perhaps, you were cured.

They had watched television, then gone to bed. He wanted to make love, though it was not quite that. He wanted to be made love *to*. He thought that she would sense it, but instead she began to talk again, began to ask whether it was his divorce that was troubling him – to insist, in her way, that it was. But it was not that. He was surprised at how little it was that.

She eventually fell silent. After a time she turned away, as if to sleep. When he asked her whether something was wrong, she said nothing. Soon they began to argue. After a time he got up, put on his clothes, and went to collect some things from the living-room, making as if to leave. One word would have stopped him, one plea, but even when he re-passed the door she said nothing. The book had been there. Something had snapped.

Out on the veranda he was momentarily halted by the hugeness of the night after the cramped rooms of the house. He felt in his pocket for the keys of the car – her car – but then, disgusted at the gesture, reached instead for his bicycle. The dog came out from its place by the lantana and yawned as he wheeled down the path and out through the gate. Once on the asphalt he rode quickly up to the highway and then steadily into a warm breeze from the east, at once trying to outpace a feeling of his own ridiculousness and rejoicing in the freedom of the wind and the dark, broad road, finding in his exertion an outlet at last for the anger that all night had twisted within him. Still it was directed at Kate, at her selfishness, her final refusal to speak. Why, at the time he most needed them, did women always turn inward, as if shocked that he could falter? Why did they turn away, saying nothing, claiming that nothing was wrong?

There were very few cars on the highway, and few lights still burning in the houses that he passed. He tried to guess what time it was and sensed that, behind him somewhere, the huge yellow moon was setting or had already gone. As he turned from the main thoroughfare into the smaller streets that led to his own, he began to think that this had happened too often, that it could be his opportunity to end the relationship. Always he had gone from tie to tie. Now, perhaps, he could work, could concentrate, could enjoy properly the freedom and options of a single being.

As he climbed the last and highest hill before the descent towards his own apartment, feeling the breeze now cooler and the atmosphere cleaner in the tree-lined streets, he began to think of how he had left her, to see her silence not as stubbornness but as confusion, bewilderment at this sudden anger. What mattered, as he reached the summit and began the descent towards the river, was not how much she withheld, but how much she had given, not what she talked about, but what she might have and did not.

As he entered his apartment the heat of the night and his exertion struck him suddenly. He took off his shirt and reached immediately for the telephone, noting the time as her number rang. But for his stupidity they might have had an hour's sleep by now. He let it ring out – twenty-five signals – and rang again. Still she did not answer. There was too much to say – to apologize for – to leave it like this. There seemed nothing to do but to ride back.

Outside, retracing his path, he found that his mind had cleared. Some sort of crisis had passed, leaving him receptive to the things around him, the rhythms of the machine. The air rushed in his ears. Beneath the regular soft sigh of his pedalling, there was a hum of tyres on bitumen, a rapid tick of ball-bearings in the axle. He thought now not so much of Kate as of the strangeness of the argument itself. The old astrologers had been correct. There were rhythms inside the body – stars, planets in orbit, cycles and eclipses – and what if they overlapped, what if a body's solstice coincided with a solstice outside? It *was* the solstice, or must nearly be, and the moon, too, had been full. How many in the city today, or out here in the dark suburbs, might have been in their grip? How many others were feeling the frenzy pull them – a conspiracy, a whirlpool, a vortex sucking them in?

On the rise before the highway he heard the shouts of

children. Concerned that they should be out at this hour, he stopped and tried to follow the sound. He was surprised to find that it came, not from behind, but from high up in the great gums that leaned out over the streetlights from the park beside him, and that it was not a crowd of children but a huge flock of white cockatoos, several on every branch he could see. Inexplicably awake and murmuring together, they sounded like a distant schoolyard. He looked around to see if there were anyone else to watch this thing, and it was then that he noticed, on the wide lawn beneath the trees, the bed of roses, red, pink and orange in the cadmium light, too strong and deliberate for coincidence.

He knocked softly on the door, then twisted the stiff, old bell, that grated rather than rang. In the silence following he felt the hard driving of his heart after the ride, and the sweat as it trickled from his shoulders towards the small of his back. Soon he heard a soft shuffling inside and glimpsed a shadowy movement behind the frosted glass. The door opened a few inches, and then further, and she led him in. She was naked, and for a moment he held her and felt the heat of her body. Moving back slightly in the dark, she fumbled at his belt, began wordlessly to undress him. He groped for his saddle-bag and the roses, mumbling at the same time a confused complaint at her not answering the telephone, at the ride, at the rose thorns that still stung his fingers.

They moved through the curtained living-room into the moonlit kitchen. While he poured himself water from a bottle in the refrigerator she arranged in its thin white light the crushed blooms in a glass. From the slowness of her movements, her unsteadiness, he realized that she had been sleeping deeply.

In the dark heat of the bedroom she turned to him, touching him at last, stroking his chest, sobbing quietly. He felt rough, unfinished, too large and too crude for what he wanted to offer. He tried to find words, but all the possibilities seemed too trite, too loud for the room.

'Did you pick up the book?' he asked at last, although he had seen that it no longer lay where he had thrown it.

'Yes.'
'Was it all right?'
'Yes.'

It was almost five. The dog's bark at something on the street had woken him and he felt alert, unable to sleep. It was still dark, though in the east there was already a thin crust of blue. Thirsty, he rose carefully and made his way to the kitchen. In the light from the open refrigerator he caught sight of the roses on the sill where she had left them. Although so roughly torn from their bushes and thrust into his saddlebag, in the blue dark for hours already they had been settling, recomposing, and were now more full and more real than he could ever have imagined, the lustre of their petals as rich and heavy as the nap of velvet, with velvet's frosting, its faint inner shine. Above their large brown thorns they were unfurling, exposing their softness, their wound-coloured hearts. The circles of their petals, large and open at the periphery, tightened towards the centre, and the deep red of one, like the pink of the other, was strident, almost violent, and preternaturally beautiful. Their boldness, their easy, unconscious complexity disarmed him. But above all it was the passionate calm, the unearthly blazing stillness, that had been going on, arranging, strengthening, all the time that he had been asleep.

The Tape-Recorders of Dreams

First came writing, then movable type. After a shorter period –
although again it was a long, long time – the flat-bed and treadle
platen gave way to huge, electrically driven monsters. It was a
kind of watershed: not only the written, but the spoken soon
could be recorded, and next the image of those who spoke it.
Soon pictures began to move – jerkily, too rapidly at first, but
then, as sound caught up with them, slowing to a more natural
gait. We could hear ourselves on prickly drums, or see ourselves
moving, at the outset as if through a sepia fog, and then in black
and white, and then, at last, in colour.

It was not long before you could do this all yourself: tape-
recorders for your voice, and videos, the tape-recorders of the
eyes, for things and faces. Machines began to reproduce,
transmit and understand in ways we'd never have thought
possible. Suddenly, it seemed, you could telephone a friend
and watch them on a screen before you; you could go to a little
booth outside a bank and talk into a wall as if it knew you.

This last, a kind of voice-imprinting, was revolutionary I
suppose, perhaps even the turning-point, but in an age of
revolutions it had been seen, as was all else, as principally a
matter of time. So too, it was only a matter of time before we
had such gadgets in the home; appliances that operated on
command, typewriters that printed as you spoke. Those who
looked backwards, it may be, suffered a kind of future-shock,
but to those of us who looked only forwards all of this seemed
quite natural. If voices could be read, then why not thoughts?
If conscious thoughts, then why not those of the unconscious
mind?

So it was, in any case, we came to the tape-recorders of dreams, huge things at the start, but eventually so small that you could put them on your bedside table.

The effects upon the lives of those who used them were at first extraordinary. Things which had long lain hidden in sleep became suddenly open to the waking mind; alternate characters emerged which were and yet were not oneself; one found oneself in possession of a passion, or capable of violence, that one would never have admitted or condoned. Yet one was forced to allow that all these things lurked somewhere deep within one, a welter of inconceivable obsessions and neuroses, offering themselves up for contemplation and analysis from far below the calmest surfaces.

Although the face of society was not thus greatly altered, one's judgements upon its extremities were dramatically curtailed. One had to admit that deep within one's self was very likely, in embryo, all evil, all perversity, and so one trod all the more gingerly, all the more grateful than one had been before for the apparent restraint of those who might point a finger. And if, to some, it was in this way as if a dredge had lifted from the bottom of a silted harbour an oozing load of the most unutterable filth and corruption, to others it was as if a pleasure-box, a casket of unimaginable jewels, had been opened within them: love blossomed in dreams that had never blossomed before; fulfilments were offered that, waking, had never yet been possible.

Only a few, of course, had dreams of such extremity, although many others found their night-time journeys equally perplexing. To some, for example, it was, instead, as if they had entered a wilderness of puzzles, untraceable mazes, inexplicable interminglings of the bizarre and the familiar, a world made up of desperate chases, frantic pursuits through labyrinths of paths and tunnels, upon obscure missions, to ends never fully revealed. (To others, a small minority, forever unaware of their complicity, it was to be staggering, over and again, across a snow-covered ski slope amidst tall, dark pines, the air about them shredded with screams, the night sky reddened by flames from a white chalet.)

But to most it was only, at last, one's ordinary life distorted, the unfinished business of the days before completed, albeit in unlikely ways, amongst familiar faces, unromantic scenes: interminable conversations, cross-examinations, tests passed or failed or obsessively sat and re-sat, seductions continually interrupted at almost the point of consummation, the suppressed anxieties of the waking life played out in gross hyperbole, with variations that, although initially absurd, proved always to be, in only thin disguise, some connection with some other ordinary current of one's life. These dreamers, perhaps, were those whose tapes soonest lay idle, or else were faithfully replayed each day, not in pursuit of resolution, but as a kind of soap opera whose characters and sets were only more familiar and affective than the others.

To some, however – my real subjects – these machines became a tool of far more vital consequence, attractive to the deepest levels of their beings. And what havoc they played there! Such people – victims, thinkers – formed for a time a kind of spiritual vanguard, their speculations touching on our most fundamental preconceptions.

By such, that is to say, it came to be suggested that at death we are not transported to some new and unaccustomed place, but into that parallel world towards which our dreams had always gestured. The afterlife, they held, was not, as we might once have thought, a Heaven or a Hell, so much as a continuous fluctuation between alternate and interdependent states of lives and of desires we already knew. If this perpetual alternation in itself was Hell, or seemed as if it might become so, then it entailed, of course, no dire alteration of our existing metaphysics, but it seemed to these people just as likely that the one state would always make the other seem like Hell, or Heaven, and vice versa. It was evident, in any case, that if this were true, and if, in death, one were catapulted into the realm of what had been one's dreams to find that they all suddenly cohered, it would be to find also that, in that new state, sleeping after a day of the dream-life now become real, one sometimes dreamt, and that the dreams bore an uncanny resemblance to something one seemed to have known before.

An existence was thus envisioned that, unlike the one we had thought we had, encompassed innumerable lifespans, in each succeeding one of which we simply moved from one half to the other of our sleep-divided being, what had been submerged in the dreams of one now surfacing while the other, as if the far end of a see-saw, slipped from the real into the waters of dream. Or, perhaps, there were not innumerable lifespans, but only two, in a fixed and inflexible relation that, without the help of these miraculous machines, we might never have realized, and so might never have been able to transcend.

There evolved swiftly, in this manner, a kind of School of Eternal Recurrence, its adherents, those haggard victims of the inner gaze, people who spent much of their waking life in the replaying and analysis of their sleeping – seeking, some said, removal from this supposed perpetual vacillation between one and the other of their greater lives quite simply by reducing the one to a state of constant contemplation of the other. The one life, it was held, gained thus the more substance, the more reality, by becoming the constant focus of the other which, in its turn, had the compass of its independent being reduced almost to naught. On the one hand there would come about a dreamless reality, and on the other a realityless dream, their interdependence broken, the vacillation over, the dream-machines falling eventually silent in a rain of grey-white snow.

This was one party, in any case, but there were others, chief amongst them that of the *voyageurs* or seekers of doors, who believed that the dream-life and the waking were not complementary, but alternating stages of a continuing outward trajectory. In everyone's dream-tapes, they claimed, there could be found somewhere a door upon which the dreamer knocked, or was about to knock, and which was never opened, or a tunnel one did not pass through, a street or passage one did not venture down. These streets and doors and passages, if penetrated, could give access to another life, the further streets and doors and passages within the dreams of which would in turn give on to other, yet more different lives in a potentially unending congeries. If some of this sect argued that this chain, this zig-zag of lives, led up towards eventual enlightenment, and others that it took one simply outwards and away, all at least were united in the firm belief that there were not two lives between which we perpetually vacillated, but so many and so different that the selves which we became might never recognize the selves from which they had become.

Periods of technological advancement come and go. Hopes that the dream-machines might have been eclipsed by some further invention, which might, perhaps, have helped to solve the riddles that they had created, appear to have been ill-founded. Although, alas, this is no longer an age of revolutions, politics too have played their part, setting back sometimes by decades our research in such directions. Governments by turns have banned or promoted the tape-recorders of dreams. There were even, once, at a time of particular unrest, gangs of self-righteous realists who sought to smash all such machines they found. The present government seems to have no particular policy concerning the matter. Although it's true that often on buses or in theatre queues or walking about in public places one encounters the pale and vacant gaze of those addicted to the tape-recordings of their dreams, it may be that, at last, society has assimilated the invention and moved on – aided, perhaps, by a growing conviction amongst the intelligentsia that the competing sects, with their conflicting explanations, were but a new incarnation of an ancient philosophical dispute, each side of which presented an argument that carried in its belly its own opposite, those who conceived of the dream-lives as moving ever outward and away condemned to find, at the furthest extremity of the congeries, that they become themselves again, and those who saw the dream and waking lives as complementary and interdependent, in seeking to overcome that interdependence, moving ever outwards and away.

Disappearing

The sudden, total disappearance of Professor R. came as a shock to all of us. Not really the disappearance as such, but the abruptness, the completeness of it. Few of us had ever thought that Being itself might require vigilance: one had always *been*, would *be* until carried away by accident or natural causes. Besides, there was always so much else to think about – so many forms, so many meetings to attend, so many exigencies of the shore to prevent one ever straying into such waters.

Although we had never talked about it (that, doubtless, was part of the problem!), and although few of us might actually have thought of it as such, we had all, at some time or another, experienced some kind of fading, or known someone who had. But it had always been a sense not so much of vanishing as of a gradual diminution of substance, a lightening: people would brush past one on the stairs, for example, and there would not be the expected apology; doors would become heavier, harder to open; one might think one had been seeing less and less of a certain colleague, and yet, paradoxically, one had seen him quite regularly, only there had been less and less of him to see.

I myself remember especially one long, hot staff-meeting two years ago. I had been watching one man in particular, my colleague S., increasingly intrigued, as a fly battered the corners of the windows and the voices droned on incessantly, by the manner in which his skin seemed slowly to be taking on the pale, grey-yellow of the wall behind him. Suddenly, with no small shock, I realized that I was beginning to see the wall *through* him, perceiving, as the meeting wore on, the line of his chair-back becoming, taking over, the line of his shoulders. I removed my glasses surreptitiously and pressed my fingers to my eyes, but the effect continued, ceasing only when the meeting closed and, in the coolness of the balcony, a cigarette and change of background returned to him something of his former self.

Slowly, with careful observation, cued by a few such incidents, I began to be able to trace a process. Someone might attend every meeting, might sit in the same place at the long, polished table, blowing out the same cigarette smoke at the same regular intervals, drawing the same doodles, but, because their appearance, their interjections, the patterns of their activity never changed, would slowly become absorbed into the dusky barrenness of the space, would begin, for the rest of us, to exist no more than does a piece of furniture when it is not watched, not needed. And yet, of course, when needed, a piece of furniture can be called back, whereas retrieval of the human, I suspect, is far more difficult, a far less certain process.

As so often happens, once I had noticed this phenomenon in one of its forms, I began to notice it in many: B., for example, who became almost indistinguishable from his own rose garden; L., who became a kind of human cricket bat; or the even stranger case of C., once brilliant, who seemed to find, at last, all new ideas too heavy for his tongue to lift, too convoluted for his eyes to wade through, and eventually, in the annual repetition of his ancient lectures, became little more than a human gramophone, the words becoming less and less distinct, the messages eventually disappearing in the irreversible attrition of their factness.

C.'s case, I must admit, was one of the sadder, and yet I cannot help but feel that, held before the mind, it might be found the most indicative of the true causes, not only of disappearance in general, but of the most disturbing case of all, the bizarre evaporation of Professor R.

Could it be that one begins to live so much within certain assumptions that they take one over, that one eventually lives so little outside them that, whenever one of them is challenged, whenever there is a trembling in these foundations, a portion of the self is lost?

On the surface, as it happened, R.'s disappearance was quite different: here was no fading of outline, no increasing pallor (quite the opposite!), and if you had tried, at different times, to lift him bodily from the ground, you would only have found him heavier and heavier. But I am now convinced that something of the kind was happening – that, despite the outward signs, some sort of disappearing was, if not in progress, at least in preparation.

Now that he is gone, of course, there are some who claim to have noticed for some time a certain fragility, a lack of his older stridency, a thinness of conversation in his recent years. One has even gone so far as to suggest that, could he have painted the landscape of the professor's mind, it would not have been the rugged jungle of his floreat, but something flat and broad and even, with no dark places, little vegetation, few signs of life or water.

One can always think such things in retrospect; the truth is that there was no clear warning. All that is known is that, on a certain Friday, after his usual committee meeting, R. entered his office and was never seen again. The authorities, it seems, cannot interpret such spontaneous evaporation as anything but abduction, suicide or murder. They have interviewed numerous suspects and potential witnesses, myself included. Descriptions, too, have been sent throughout the country. And yet the signs, I think, are there for all to see.

I had not been into R.'s office for some time – few had – but life goes on; it had to be cleared, and I, as one who had at one time known him well, was deputized to go through certain papers. They were not there. Nor was it the office I remembered. The room, once cluttered and untidy, now had a spartan simplicity. Almost all of the books and files, the photographs and statuettes had gone, and in their place, where once large shelves had been, were now only a poster and a simple mirror, the latter strange because, of all of us, I would have thought R. to have been the least concerned with his appearance, and the former – of a vast mudflat; the bottom of a newly vanished lake, perhaps – no less perplexing.

On the lake, far out, but stark against the towering mountains, was a small silver figure, clad much like an astronaut. In its hands was a small box which it seemed to be pointing towards the dry, caked surface. I stared at it a long time, though whether, then, I was thinking much about it I cannot say. Nor can I really say whether, as I thought at the time, it was the faint sound of a cicada that brought me back to the room, or whether I brought that sound back with me. I was, in any case, almost half-way down the stairs, fumbling absentmindedly for my car keys, before I realized that, as I closed the door, the poster still in the corner of my eye, the tiny, helmeted figure had begun to move.

The Family of the Minister

The minister was one of his country's success stories. Born in a tiny river village, he had, like most of his generation, escaped as soon as he was able, leaving as far as he could behind him the heat and dirt, the drone of insects and the dung and sweat of animals. In the city he had worked at first as a road labourer, and then at a succession of jobs – factory worker, mechanic, carpet-layer – until starting his own small business. At thirty, to the amazement of many who knew him, he was almost a millionaire.

Money, however, did not quite satisfy as he'd expected. He had been tempted rather easily into politics. It had not been a mistake: the postwar years were particularly good to a vigorous and ambitious still-young man with so wide a range of experience, and he had impressed. His party had needed someone who could appeal to farmers and factory workers, to small and big business alike. By forty-two he had been given a minor portfolio, and then, at fifty, the Ministry of the Interior.

Denise helped greatly. Ten years younger, she had come from a similar background, with a determination even stronger than the minister's to obliterate its traces. Since meeting him she had begun to realize her dreams with a kind of ruthless efficiency. She it was who furnished and redecorated, and who ensured that, item by item, all the essential purchases were made. She it was who, when their social position seemed at last to demand it, ensured that all the appropriate staff were employed.

Where the two children fitted into this was never very clear, at least to outsiders. To some they seemed just further dictates of Denise's dreams, along with dishwashers, with second cars, with wall-to-wall pile carpeting – an excuse, perhaps, for decades more of acquisition as each passed through successive stages of their childhood and youth. Yet clearly the minister and his wife loved Alice and Michael with a passion.

All, in a sense, seemed perfect. The minister, when his schedule allowed, could barricade himself with his loved ones in a house of maximum convenience, a brick-and-tile cornucopia, looking whenever he wished through ample windows onto carefully manicured lawns, and gardens in which everything grew almost exactly to order. If sometimes protesters gathered at the gates, their chants could barely be heard over the high stone walls, and if ever, as did sometimes happen, the press wished to photograph or he were required, on little notice, to receive at home a foreign delegation, he could lead them through reception rooms and rose garden with perfect confidence that nothing would ever be amiss.

And yet it was. It was hardly something an infrequent visitor would see, though more than one cook or housemaid had become somewhat uneasy. The lawns, they might have said, were not so much cultivated as repressed, the gardens oppressively symmetrical. In that climate, too, whole armies of insects marched on every household, yet here, in the minister's residence, nothing of that kind stirred. The cupboards revealed instead a disagreeable array of baits and poisons, flysprays and repellants, air-fresheners and deodorants as if, not content with walls and military order, the family must set up a sort of chemical barrier to the world.

In their behaviour, too, there was something a little disturbing, if sometimes also slightly ridiculous. On picnics, for example, of which, as matters of form, there were always one or two a year, the son would take a portable television and the daughter an array of table games, as if the purpose were not to enjoy the open air, but to distract oneself from it. On such occasions the parents too seemed ill at ease, Denise protesting profusely at the heat or flies, the minister wandering about listlessly or sitting in an empty-handed daze.

Nor was it very easy to say which member of the family was most particularly affected. The maids could have told stories of all of them. Once, during a long wet summer, when half the cleaning staff had been away, Alice had found a tiny mushroom growing on the grouting in a corner of her bathroom, and had taken to her bed for the rest of the day. Another time, when Denise had insisted upon showing the cook the way to best prepare an omelette, she had cracked a fertilized egg into a green porcelain bowl, and had not only fled the room to vomit, but had refused all food for a week.

A hatred of nature, perhaps, but it was not that exactly. True, there was always a faint disgust, a concerted endeavour to keep it at bay, but there was also about the whole family an air of innocent vacancy, an almost complete lack of malice that was, for many, as endearing as it was disturbing – a sense, maybe, that their actions and opinions were not eventually their own, that all four were in the grip of something larger.

One night, sitting by the television, Alice had been absent-mindedly fingering the fold behind her ear, and had found something rough there, something not her. A little dry skin, of course, and so slight as to be hardly noticeable. But it was not that. A closer examination, during a commercial break, revealed tiny whorls and leaf-like forms, and a grey-green colour unlike anything but lichen – that had fallen from a tree, perhaps, and lodged in her hair. Or might have, if it had not happened again.

And then the earwigs in her study. At first only in the remoter places – seams of the curtains, behind books on the upper shelves – but coming, closer and closer. The slaters, too, not under a rock, or beneath an old paper left rotting in the garden, but inside, on a seat from which she had only just risen. The more she touched, the more the lichen grew; the more she looked, the more insects she saw, as if the touching, the looking somehow exacerbated what they found. And yet the process had begun, and was soon a morbid fascination: hate it as she might, she *would* touch, *would* look, and nothing could prevent it.

Whether or not, on the other hand, something might have prevented the change in Michael's arm no one could say. By the time it was discovered – months after the break, as the pin was being removed – the bone had the texture, the fibrosity of wood, and the process seemed irreversible. Once again, the appropriate connections were not made. The condition was related only too readily to something in the break itself, and 'woodiness' was only metaphor. Alice, it's true, might have spoken up, but shame is a wonderful censor, and to suggest some kind of link, had she seen it, would have been to admit not only to lichens, or a perplexing plague of lice and earwigs and slaters, but to persistent hints of fungus, and a mould too intimate or humiliating for speech.

The parents were no more perceptive. If connections were made, they were personal only, and did not extend to the others. There was, for example, the minister's own skin affliction, at first diagnosed as eczema or incipient psoriasis, although he soon began to decipher more. It began, that is, as shark or leatherjacket, and then become worse. Not all over, by any means, but in small, itchy patches on knees and elbows, and creeping slowly down the limbs. He found that, if he was careful, if he kept it moist, it was not always noticeable. If he never wore shorts or rolled his sleeves, if he always cleaned away the tell-tale scales, he might almost learn to live with it.

Indeed, it was amazing what one could come to tolerate in time. A duodenal ulcer, for example, or high blood pressure, although there were occasions when, the skin problem much on his mind, he found himself thinking of the one as a slow, opening flower within him, or of the other as a distant, uncanny effect of the muggy late-summer riverflats of his childhood, a place of leeches, stinging insects, dark mud oozing up between the toes. None of this – the fish-skin, the flowering gut, the muddy bloodstream – was his own. Over and again, trying to explain it to himself, he remembered how every trevally, every flathead, every bream that he had caught back then had had, clinging unmercifully to the walls of its throat, a fat, grey grub, taking its toll of every morsel that its host had eaten.

There was, also, Denise's abdomen. For months a great tiredness had troubled her, and a fluctuating pain, now strong, now weak, now localized in one place, now another. Referred pain, some doctor had called it, but she developed the eerie conviction that there was something inside her, a plant perhaps, that had begun as a seed and was growing. At times she could actually feel its roots, and a choking pressure, a debilitating fullness, as if all the available space within were being slowly occupied, as if she were being gradually taken over.

The condition, eventually, grew so severe that she could spend no more than a few hours daily out of bed. At this point, Williams-Burnett, the elderly Englishman who had treated Michael, suggested that she enter his clinic for observation. He and his colleagues conducted an ultrasound examination. Throughout the procedure, Denise asked what they were seeing, but they made only the most general of responses, attempting unconvincingly to suggest that all was in order. She tried hard to see the screen, but could glimpse it only once before they turned it away. That was enough. The things beating that she knew were not organs, the flash of something like a fin or tail.

Williams-Burnett decided against exploratory surgery: he had ruled out, it seemed, ectopic pregnancy, or a possible appendicitis. Denise, in any case, seemed to recover slightly. Certainly she did not complain of the pains any more. But night after night, in the dark beside her husband, she lay with her fingers pressed deep into her abdomen, feeling the persistent flutterings, the occasional sickly slithering. She did not tell the minister. Indeed, in the painful light of day after day, she could hardly tell herself.

When she died suddenly, and without apparent warning, Williams-Burnett was obliged to perform an autopsy. For reasons he did not disclose, he did this in secret, at his clinic, late in the evening, with special arrangements for removal of the body. It was as he'd suspected. There were things still living. It was not the first time he had encountered this, but he had hoped never to see it again.

He did not, this time, have the heart to kill them. Making sure first that the lights had gone out in the ward upstairs, he took them in a small box to the far side of the grounds, and released them into the stream. By first light, with luck, they would be far out in the harbour, making their way towards the sea.

Disease

There is a fundamental yet elusive relationship between words and things. Sometimes I think that it is the things that bring words into existence, sometimes the words that bring the things. Whichever way it is, the problem is a complex one, and defies reduction. What comes first, courage, splendour, righteousness, or their names, a disease, or the word for it? Perhaps it is neither; perhaps each is a phase, a stage in the evolution of the other, or maybe they are in a symbiotic relationship, each depending upon, each needing the other for its fulfilment.

Without doubt *some* connection, *some* interdependence is there. Whenever, for example, I see a great many words of a certain kind gathered together, or hear them, in the speeches of an orator, clustering about a particular subject in abnormal proportions, I think of the white blood cells that a body produces to combat an intruder, the sudden, super-average presence of which is taken by pathologists as evidence of disease. But again, which is it, the disease or the words that has come first? Sometimes, as I look at the evident satisfaction with which certain phrases are uttered, I wonder if perhaps a pressure of the words is there, and the disease has but provided them an object – the site, but not the true cause of their eruption. In any case it appears that, as of so much else, the seeds of an infection germinate in a bed of language.

Surely what is possible to one person might be possible to the society as a whole. I have seen my wife, upon the receipt of a certain letter, fall suddenly victim to severe stomach pains. I have seen a note barely two lines long, passed to a colleague in the middle of a meeting, produce almost instantly a devastating migraine. Words *can* become flesh, it seems, and do most certainly afflict it. Nature and language – the machine of words – may now have become so deeply entwined that no one can truly tell where one begins or where the other ends.

Please do not misunderstand me. I know that people die from identifiable physical ailments in most painful and distressing ways. Recently, indeed, I have seen an alarming number of my acquaintance waste gradually away, accompanied by a set of symptoms that, to almost all, points most directly at a common cause – pale, ghostly bruises that, like restless flowers, float a long time just beneath the skin, then, breaking through, are answered by parallel disruptions deep within, the hands becoming dry as parchment, the mind itself withdrawing, behind the frail cobwebs of the flesh, towards some zero point unreachable by speech. But where do symptoms end, or where begin? Can we truly say that when *this* and *this* and *this* have come together we have a disease, and not when *that* and *that* have joined them or have not appeared? And even when we can draw firm borders, establish clearest lines of definition, can we truly say that the assumptions, the habits of thought by which we do so have come from the thing itself, and not from our own minds, or that there are not causes behind causes, diseases beyond or beneath, of which the present is itself but symptom?

True disease, they say, when it does come, will allow no such pause. It will strike alike the humble and the proud, the vicious and the pure. There will be no advertisement; there will be little debate. It will be like a great paw of the sky seen from a bare hill by a person standing utterly alone. The righteous will suffer with the unrighteous, the strong will suffer with the weak. It will corrupt not only the physical, but the mind's body also. Those who have uttered vomit will be made to eat it; those who have never looked will be made to see unceasingly. Or else, perhaps, it will be a silent, nameless thing, a debility we do not know we have. A lightening, or slow erasure, a non-renewal of presence. The dinosaurs, I have heard it claimed, were not killed by an epidemic, as has long been thought, but by a gradual change in atmosphere, in the imperceptible face of which they did not rage or roar, but simply, as the generations passed, became more tired, less definite, weaker and weaker.

Maybe, one day, they will call these the New Plague Years, although as they are happening we are not so sure. The disease – if indeed it is such a thing at all – takes so many different forms. Only a few, it seems, suspect their connection, or realize that, after all, we are all suffering from the same distress, the same probable cause.

There are the sexual varieties, for example, but is sex their only origin? Maybe, as many have suggested, there is in all of this something of the vengeance of God, but what *is* God? Certainly no elderly, hirsute gentleman. Certainly no gentleman! A dream of ourselves, perhaps, but if we live in the same dream too long? If it hardens about us into a suit so inflexible, so impermeable that our very bodies cannot breathe? At a party once, a splendid, decadent affair at the colonial governor's, there entered, at the height of the festivities, a thoroughly naked man and woman, painted all over in shining black. For almost an hour – their eyes, their open mouths, their sexual parts vivid against the darkness of their bodies – they delighted and scandalized everybody there. But then collapsed. As the paint had dried, as its shining surface had lost its porosity, their skin had been less and less able to breathe. They took first the woman, and then the man away, but nothing could be done.

At that time, the time also of all the excited activity just before the first uprising, there broke out in the artists' quarter a strange new affliction, mild but persistent, annoying but never quite debilitating. Misdiagnosed, it spread quickly amongst us and then, in a sense, was all but forgotten, or became a part of our lives. Remaining strong, remaining active, with so much political confusion to distract us, how could we worry about so small a thing? And yet soon there were headlines, articles, voices in every medium condemning us, in all our innocence, as the instigators of epidemic, as carriers of a new and insidious leprosy.

Almost overnight, attention was focused upon us in a manner none of us could ever have envisioned. And yet at first it was rarely upon individuals, almost always upon the affliction itself. Those of us who had received it early, who had been originally misdiagnosed, remained unknown to anyone unless we came voluntarily forward. It was an inner burden only, a matter of individual conscience. This in particular must have annoyed the authorities. As if specifically to flush us out, stories circulated ever more widely as to tragic side effects, gruesome case studies received national exposure. It became difficult, at the height of this campaign, to go anywhere without hearing, somehow or another, of the evil that we carried with us.

At first, the effect of such publicity was devastating. More than one of us broke down or committed suicide, too ashamed to admit, even amongst what was left behind, the true cause of our despair. Even now, as if it were etched in my brain, I can see the image of Elise, my lover then, standing naked in our bedroom, racked by a wild and uncontrollable sobbing at the thought that she had at last contracted the condition from me. And yet, as we learnt to live with our supposed curse, such rumours of dire consequence proved groundless. More than one of us began to suspect that their true nature had been political, a means of isolating us, an attempt, by the government, to taint and discredit a troublesome opposition. And eventually, I think, it was this, not any syringe, that immunized us; it was from this, not from any invasion of the bodily tissues, that we drew whatever antibodies we have.

Aware as we were then – as we still are so many years later – that if we allowed our condition to be known we would become pariahs, we were condemned instead to live two lives, to play a game and yet to know its unreality. Sitting at a fashionable dinner, for example, hearing that condition – our own – discussed in the foulest and most frightening terms by guests who had believed what they had heard, we would become aware, again and again, of a skein of ironies that could become almost unbearable. And yet, of course, we could carry on, feigning an ignorance, mouthing a prejudice we could not share.

What began as a defence became a habit of mind. On a platter of our own afflicted flesh, we had been given a clue, a vital key: lied about, we began to suspect the ubiquity of lies; denied speech, we became adept in the arts of subterfuge. As if a set of upended dominoes had begun to fall or we had become amphibious, living at once within the world we had known and also in the vast, uncharted sea surrounding it, soon every notion, every reported truth had its shadow, every fact came with its own small retinue of those that had been silenced that it might be heard. Disease, which might have been only the suffering of the body, only the burden of the individual mind, became dis-ease with all that we had known, and our past reality instead a stage, a dancing-floor, a small, illusory platelet of apparent light created by the random intersection of currents in a great, circumambient night.

It must also be said that beneath this a stranger, moral alchemy occurred. Slowly, yet indisputably, the very guilt we had begun with became transformed. What had been at first our shame became a power we might never otherwise have had, and the affliction itself a dark gift, bestowing upon those we loved, *because* we loved (for they were those most certainly infected), the possibility of a second sight, a lens that might condense into sudden, stark relief, the unsuspected interdependencies of love and cruelty, sex and death, condemning its carriers to live within and judge by the black lights of a knowledge from which the day-to-day had hitherto protected them.

And now, of course, there is the new disease, with its mysterious, almost unspeakable relation to the old. By what strange power its manifold components have been brought together from the places where they might have lurked for centuries no one can say. As always, there are those insisting that its cause is somehow written in its symptoms, yet no virologist can confidently classify it, no epidemiologist has seen its kind before.

Through all the incompatible analyses, the apparent bewilderment of medicine, however, there are those of us who have begun to suspect one most intriguing, most disturbing factor – that those whom the first disease has made amphibious, for whom the dominoes have long ago begun to fall, are almost certainly immune. While this is a source of great relief, it is also, paradoxically, the source of our greatest anxiety. What is it, exactly, that gives us such protection? Is it that our own affliction has in fact been, as we have come to think of it, a mark or source of health, and that it is its very presence in us that wards off the new? Or is it not our own condition as such, but the antibodies it has produced in us, that gives us our defences? If it is the latter, then is not our own disease somehow a harbinger, a cause of this, and our exemption a sign, not of our innocence, but of the deepest complicity?

War has been declared, of course, and the fire-wardens and recruiting sergeants are out, thrilled by the chance to defend all they hold dear. They do not realize how much it is their own hysteria that defines their enemy, or that it is the very strength of their reaction that determines the territory occupied. Far from the careful, clinical catalogue of symptoms everywhere so brutally displayed, the true public shape of the new affliction resembles nothing so much as a portrait, in negative, of our own society, black where the latter would be most white, blank or indifferent where it would be most black.

As in our own case, twenty years ago, first one group then another has been blamed, but the new affliction in every instance has refused to be contained. By far its largest strain, it seems, again is sexually transmitted, but precisely when, and how, with what incubation, what triggering factors is not known. Far from following a clear, predictable path, it leap-frogs, breaks out as if spontaneously in the least expected places, tracing histories – of shame and transgression, desire and its fulfilment – that none had yet suspected or dared to admit. So many of the purest, the most chaste amongst us have been struck down that few, if any, can be sure they do not have its seed within them, or that it did not enter years ago, before the thing itself was ever given name.

The boundaries have become confused, the outcry has only fanned the flames. Not only is it no longer possible to predict whom next the malady will strike, but we cannot say with any certainty just what it is our friends and neighbours are succumbing to. Is the disease, if that is what it is, a sufficient, or merely an efficient cause? Are the symptoms that we see truly those of the thing itself, or only of the mind's reaction to publicity?

The chill grows wider. For all the dry midsummer weather, the heat that many fear will stimulate this thing beyond all possible control, there is, within almost all of us, an uneasy cold, a kind of festering winter. Where once, on a bus, in a street, a restaurant, to meet the eye of an attractive stranger was an adventure, people now look away like frightened animals. The hint of interest or desire is like a veiled threat of death, and cannot be thought of without it.

This is not new. Sexuality has always been an analogue, an ally of dis-ease, and now the body has become its metaphor. When all the current trouble is surveyed, I wonder how many there will be who see the uncanny resemblance of this new affliction to the last, and who, placing symptom by symptom, disease by disease, can work their way deeper, further in, towards something more fundamental than we have yet suspected – an ancient god, perhaps, but it is not quite that – before which we now stand like exhausted explorers who have come upon a huge and unimagined monument. And, right and left, are hesitating, turning back, dying, because we do not know what else to do.

Nadia's Lover

For most of us, the real is the life of the surface, the patina, the visible meniscus. But for some, far below, it must be something quite different, lived under a pressure many would find intolerable, fed, as are some of the deepest sea creatures, by the discarded and decaying matter that drifts slowly and inevitably downward, fathom after fathom, into their inconceivable dark.

The story of Nadia and Christine is like that, in some respects, but it is also not. Depth is relative; surface varies with angle of vision. What may, to many, seem almost impossible – like the greatswallowers, the lantern fish that, dragged too quickly to the surface, collapse in the sudden thinness of the atmosphere, all structure and all meaning gone – may seem to others only too familiar. We live by surfaces – interpret, read by them – yet reality itself can lie beyond at unexpected distances. It seems, in any case, as if only the simple words will do: the submarine dark, the long teeth, the grotesque, yet delicate jaws of *photostomias quernei* must be left, instead, to the oceanographer, or to those who can see a tale as something other than a casting and recasting of signs.

Nadia lived in a large house, not far from the centre of the city. It was a boarding house. In it were eleven apartments. She occupied hers, in the basement, at a much-reduced rent, in exchange for cleaning the others weekly, on Thursday and Friday, beginning with the superintendent's flat and ending with her own. The order in which she did the others did not matter, except for one, whose rooms had a particular appeal.

She had liked its location long before the present occupant moved in, and had always cleaned it late on Friday morning,

122

just before descending the long dark staircase to the airless passageways, the tiny bubble of light that was her kitchenette. This apartment – the nice one – was on the top floor, in the centre, and had by far the best view of the small park opposite, a neat, flower-bordered square hardly the size of a building lot, with benches spaced evenly among well-groomed trees. There was a small delicatessen to the left; workers from the offices would buy their lunches there and eat them on the benches in the sun. Over the low hedge that insulated them from the city traffic, Nadia could see almost perfectly.

Once, soon after she had first come here, she had looked out of the middle window. It had been lunchtime, and a sunny spring day, and she had seen the benches full of workers. Many of the younger seemed to have formed couples, and she had been instantly intrigued by the patterns and the gestures that they made. She tried to imagine the conversations they were having, and to put herself in the place of the young girls, straightening their skirts, throwing their long hair back and laughing, showing their white teeth to the sun.

She began to return here at the same time every week, and soon imagined that she could follow the course of their relationships, in the way that some who had sat together now sat elsewhere, while others, remaining paired, sat closer or further apart. One particular couple she watched more than any. Week after week they were together, amongst the first to arrive at lunchtime, and always amongst the last to leave. All through the summer she observed them becoming closer and closer, the fair girl sometimes carrying flowers, the dark-haired youth more and more attentive, less and less conscious of others.

But then something happened. One Friday the girl did not appear, and the young man sat alone. He did so the next week, and the next, and continued to come to the park well after most others had moved inside and the leaves had begun to fall. Nadia watched him carefully. Sometimes, she thought, he looked directly up at her, and for the seconds that he seemed to do so felt a lingering shock pass through her, as if they knew each other intimately.

By the time winter finally arrived she found she had developed a liking for the flat itself, and though fewer and fewer came to the park, and even the young man himself had gone, she continued to arrive at the same time, taking almost as much pleasure from simply sitting, a cup of tea in her hand, trying, if there were nothing more pressing, to reconstruct from the possessions something of the life of the occupant. Before Miss Christine it had been a retired professor, a sad, elderly man who read many books and left her a small gift at Christmas. She'd been afraid, when he died, that coming to this flat would no longer be so pleasant, but it had worked out quite differently. Christine, you could tell, was so much more sophisticated, so much less flighty than other young women, and nothing had had to change.

When Nadia first glimpsed her, two or three weeks after she had come, Christine seemed just as attractive as her clothes, her simple perfumes, the state of the apartment had already suggested – tall, slim, dark-haired, in her early twenties, with high cheekbones, large eyes, and an open and friendly expression much like Nadia's own at such an age. And the softest, palest, most perfect skin.

Week after week, then, Nadia came to this flat, finding herself each time more anxious to get there, more happy as, closing the door behind her, she looked around, deciding where to start – checking first, perhaps, the waste-paper bins, the mantel and desk-top, the bedside table for the odd cup or glass or bread-and-butter plate. There is always a method in the way one cleans, particularly if one does so much of it, and Nadia liked to begin with raised surfaces, the obvious, and then move down, only at last, after the washing-up, the tidying of clothes, the plumping of cushions, coming to the vacuuming, the changing of bedlinen, the scrubbing and polishing and making shine. The order varied slightly from apartment to apartment: you could tell things about people's lives from their patterns of disarrangement, their habits of untidiness, the things they cast off.

Often, there was little else to do *but* tell. True, you could put on the radio, the television, but they slowed you down and Nadia was always keen to reach the top floor. She relied, instead, on the task at hand to talk to her – that is, she didn't call it talking, but might well have. In the twenty minutes spent scrubbing a kitchen or a bathroom floor, in a quarter-hour cleaning out cupboards, in the time taken to sweep behind a refrigerator or check the little valley behind the bookshelf for the papers that sometimes fell there, one noticed things, found objects people didn't know they'd lost, or might not call lost if they knew. And in the comparative silence of bristles grinding against tiling, the monotony of your own panting as, on hands and knees, you grubbed out an awkward crack, each little discovery was like an act of speech. You couldn't help but listen and add up. The stories that you followed this way, even if rarely very exciting, made it easier to come back, week after week, turning as they did the menial into a serial, a thing of instalments.

Not that Nadia was so attentive in all apartments, or that Christine's was ever far from spotless, but even spotlessness spoke or, in whispering only, left the more room for daydream. It was the spotlessness, in any case, and only occasionally – after a cup of tea, and less and less frequently a glance through the window at the empty park – the dreaming, that Nadia would take down the staircase to her own dim rooms, which always, by late afternoon, she could look at and, seeing them faintly shining – seeing them glimmer in the eddying dusk – try somehow to compare.

Perhaps it was to make this comparison the more easily that the first of her copying began – a shifting of chairs, a table, the television, to match a template above. The pursuit of a deeper spotlessness, it may be, or a lost youthfulness, although on the day when, stooping beside the bedhead, Nadia drew from the space behind it a photograph that, after an examination of several seconds, she put again where she had found it, one might have suspected more. Certainly when, three weeks later, having observed it to have gathered dust again, she picked it up and, brushing it carefully, placed it in the pocket of her apron.

For the time being – and though it might stretch the term – that was the greatest of her borrowings. Little more need be said of it, having suggested enough already to locate the photograph exactly, behind the bedhead, in a flat three floors below.

I would like instead to speak of a period some six weeks later. Christine now had a lover. At least, that is what certain facts – the occasional fair hair on the furniture and pillows, a greater disarray of bedsheets – suggested to Nadia. She was disturbed. It was the first time that her reading had conflicted so strongly with desire. When she cleaned Christine's apartment it was, for several Fridays, with a disinterest beneath which, could we probe so far, we might have found a certain earnestness. She tidied quickly, with the television on, and rarely lingered over details – until one day when, coming home, she froze in the doorway, muttering a few shocked syllables in her native Russian, having thought suddenly of someone who did not exist, who cleaned her own apartment without knowing its occupant, who read the signs she, Nadia, had left as she herself read those of others.

The signs of Christine's lover were few – a pair of her panties, crumpled deep within the bedclothes, a piece of bitten, nicotine-stained nail too large to have come from her delicate fingers – but from now on they were meticulously collected. There were things, of course, too intimate, too difficult to reproduce, and these Nadia regretfully discounted. There were also secrets of bedsheets, ambiguities of hair or odour, too slight or painful to long contemplate. But all the larger signs, all those which might catch the unskilled eye, were carefully transplanted. She wondered, sometimes, if she should feel guilty: there are things, after all, which should always be thrown away. But it was a feat, an accomplishment, to keep such a careful untidiness fresh, as if she had not yet time for it, as if her lover had just gone.

And then, one day, there was a letter, an envelope slipped under the door some time between Christine's morning departure and Nadia's arrival. It was sealed, and no name was written upon it – obviously, if it were from a lover, if it were a question of such intimacy, there would be no need for one. With some trepidation – this would be, after all, more than a borrowing – Nadia put this, too, in her pocket, and when she arrived home placed it carefully against the skirting-board where someone, emerging from the basement dark, might accidentally have kicked it, or the door itself have swept it upon opening. It seemed to Nadia, as she put it there, that this was almost the final touch, that if she were to borrow much more the tale itself might begin to seem less credible.

As if to concur with her, the signs in Christine's apartment ceased. For two or three weeks Nadia looked for them, but with decreasing fervour. Once again it was only Christine that she read. She was just beginning to think this, after all, a better state of things when suddenly, in the fourth week, she entered an empty apartment. Everything – the clothes, the books, the curtains and the furniture – had gone. All that remained, in the bleak, late-winter light that now seemed to flood through the wide, bare window, were the indentations of the table-legs and the bookshelf in the carpet, and, in the bedroom especially, the unmistakable, yet already fading scent of the one who had left.

The flat was vacant for a couple of weeks, and then occupied by an elderly woman who kept an unapproachable black cat and stayed too much at home. Nadia had to talk to her the first few times she cleaned, but then changed her routine to avoid her. By now it was spring again, and people once more lunched on the benches. Nadia sometimes watched them from a lower window, but much of the interest had gone. The young man of the year before did not return. Once or twice she wondered what had happened to him, but soon, for some reason or another, began to watch soap operas while she cleaned, and seemed, at last, to forget the park entirely.

When she cleaned her own apartment, on the other hand, it was, for a time, with particular care, as if in a sort of shrine. But even this she could not do for long. Soon, as if she too had broken with a lover, and now, at last, begun to get over it, she put her small collection in a box – the broken threads, the photograph, the unopened letter. Eventually, she thought, she would put it away in a cupboard, where some day someone, going through her things, would find it and, fingering the blond hairs, opening the envelope, would marvel that she had had such a secret, and wonder who her lover had been.

Sheep

Steven was a shepherd in the border country. It doesn't really matter *which* border, although that is something people always will ask. It might have been that between France and Spain, or that between Italy and Austria, but surely this is to speak of borders in only the narrowest sense. Might it not be just as good, for example, to say the border between Chile and Spain? For that, too, exists, if in the mind only: a high, exotic, dry and dusty frontier where scrawny creatures clamber over rocky slopes after tufts of grass under grey, blustery skies, and at night are herded into low pens of stone. It is a country, in any case, where there are valleys and mountain reaches rarely visited by outsiders, where people can be left for years without fear of intrusion, and from which only the direst thirsts need drive the shepherds into the nearest village, to sit at one of the shabby tables outside what passes for the taverna, or visit a small, whitewashed house on the outskirts where they can often stay longer than they can afford.

In this region families of necessity are small, and flocks, like land, pass in more or less unchanging size from one generation to the next. The eldest son, if ever there is more than one, inherits the land and sheep, while the younger fend for themselves, often disappearing into the city never to be seen again, or, if they are, returning only years later, in a dusty automobile, with a woman in the passenger seat, to overboil on a steep mountain track and later sit briefly over a drink at the taverna, eyeing through dark glasses the few who care to notice them as if disdaining, and at the same time begging, to be recognized.

Steven, a landless and a flockless third, had never left for the city – or, rather, had, but unlike all the others had very soon returned and never spoke of what, if anything, had happened to him there. For a time, on whatever money he could scrounge or win, he drank and whored, both in unwilling moderation. For a short time, at first, he worked in the taverna. For an even shorter time he worked on the district's largest farm. In neither place did his brooding, uncommunicative nature earn him friends, and when, upon his sudden departure from the latter, he was seen to have carried a sheep with him, there were some who said it was a fair price to be rid of him. No sheep, in any case, was found to be missing, and no pursuit was contemplated.

Nothing was heard of him for a considerable time. It was assumed that he had returned to the city (it was well known that his brothers would have nothing more to do with him). He had more or less been forgotten when, as might any other thirsty shepherd, he came into the village with a couple of lambs for sale, on the proceeds of which – they were the fattest, finest of lambs – he drank for a day and a night and a day at the taverna, and then, after sleeping off his dubious achievement in a ditch, wandered off again, early on the third morning, along the mountain road.

There was a little talk, in the days that followed, as to how he had come by the lambs he had sold, and a good deal more when it was reported, by one who had been abroad even earlier that day, that Steven, as he crested the rise outside the village, had had on his back a well-fleeced young ewe. As no one could truly say they had lost one, however, this incident, like the earlier, was soon forgotten.

It was not a ewe, but a fine stud ram, that no one saw the next time. Indeed, the whole visit went largely unnoticed, or, if known of, was known of only by those who were wont to keep such things to themselves. For this time Steven went not to the taverna, but to the small whitewashed house where, with pauses only for rest and food, he and the woman made the shapes of different animals for two nights and a day.

The pattern recurred. Sometimes Steven drank, sometimes he whored (that, at least, was how the villagers saw it), but, whichever thirst it was, he slaked it with a peculiar, almost wordless intensity, drinking more or staying longer than did any other shepherd in the area, as if, at the end of the bottle-beyond-the-last, or at the peak of the climax-beyond-exhaustion, there lay something which must be approached with the maximum of concentration. And all this, as on the first occasion, was made possible by the proceeds from the fattest of lambs. How this occurred – whence came his flock, or where he pastured it – no one could say, and, since none had missed any of their own, no one had particular reason to care.

This was perhaps just as well, for few, I'm sure, could have believed what they would have found. The villagers saw, when Steven came from the mountains, only the tip of things. He himself would have had trouble explaining. One day, while minding sheep on the large estate, he had heard a bleating from a direction from which bleating had never yet come, and at the end of it found a sheep that was no part of the flock he tended. It seemed an opportunity too good to miss. He had taken this bonus sheep and left, feeling somehow rather freer than he had ever felt before. And, far back in the mountains, in a valley too stony, too riddled with gullies, too densely wooded on the little level ground to be of use to any other shepherd, one sheep had led to another.

There seemed no other way to describe it, and Steven was glad he did not have to try. Growing up on his father's, now his eldest brother's, farm he had been taught only one way of shepherding, and had never suspected another. But here were sheep where sheep had never hidden before, and ways of finding them no longer confined to the horizontal arrangements of bush and plain, the slippery diagonals of mountain and gully-side that determined the lives of all the other shepherds he had known.

This it not to imply that Steven dug for sheep or climbed trees for them where others would have searched thickets or the rocky crags. At least, it is only partly to suggest such things. Rather, it is to say that, if some of Steven's sheep were found, as those of others might have been, by walking or by scrambling, not all of them were, and that none of them were sheep that he had known of before.

Some of them were found, that is to say, after a long day

simply thinking – simply sitting on the step of his small stone hut and contemplating the vast and placid blueness of the sky. Others were found in the deep recesses of memory, or bleating in an unguarded by-way of a dream. The strongest, the sheep of indulgence or excess, came often from his visits to the village; and if, sometimes, a sheep seemed somehow weaker than the rest, that might have been explained in part by the difficulty of the terrain that Steven had crossed to retrieve it – the fact that it came from a place so distant and so nearly intangible that the ground had almost disappeared from under him. And who was to say – or to worry – whether they were the sheep of waking when he was asleep, or the sheep of dreaming while he worked in daylight? It was all very well to think, as he did at first, that dream sheep should stay in dreams, and that only real sheep should inhabit the waking hours, but here, in this stony place in the mountains, the barriers had broken down, the fences fallen, the stock-grids, wherever there were any, clogged quickly with the mud and weed of non-reason, and who was Steven to complain, whose flock grew slowly and yet definitely larger?

Indeed, Steven had found one of his finest sheep on the day when he had come closest to explaining, as he gazed at the crazed ice on top of a puddle, how such a flock could ever have come to need such gathering. It could only have been, he had thought on this day, that some great scare, some huge catastrophe long out of mind, had sent them skittering into the corners of things, rather like the way a sudden pressure on a sopping sponge can send jets of water far and wide. But what a terrible scare it must have been, to send so many sheep into such places! And why had he been singled out to gather them?

Even this came to seem less of a question in time. Down in the village things had always been, if not idyllic, at least a little too calm and predictable, and the people too narrow and compla-cent. It seemed obvious now that he had needed the flock, as evidence of a pressure he had always felt but never had been able to pin down. It had been even worse in the city: no sheep or shepherds in the parks, no flocks even remotely suspected in the factories or public buildings, all life a matter of herding on one plane.

Here in the mountains, in any case, a new method had come to be. Steven's flock burgeoned, then stabilized. Sheep died and were replaced by others. Others, once found, were lost again. More and more the sheep of excess gave way to the sheep of wisdom. Increasingly, too, there were the black ones, the most enduring (war visited the mountains; Steven had helped the partisans). And always, had he been asked what caused this, what kept it going, he would have said, had he chosen to answer, that it was a feeling of loss, of something important missing, that there was still something somewhere that had to be found.

Not, of course, that he ever was asked – at least, not by those in the village who had come eventually to call him mad, from having lifted, one time too many, his grizzled head from the taverna table to ask him if he was all right, only to have him say, as they could never understand, *I am looking for a sheep, a bell sheep*. And at the far end of his drunkenness would often nearly find it; or after a long night and day with the woman, clambering up and down their high crags with his eyes wide open, feeling the imminent presence of the most elusive, the prize he would somehow be as disappointed as he would be overjoyed to find.

The Book

It must be called quite simply the Book, inadequate as this name sounds. It is the Book of Books, of course, but that title has already been appropriated, and I want no such confusion. 'The Book', alone, it must be. Those who know it will need no more, and there may be trouble enough convincing others that it exists at all.

Some who have possessed it have written of it at great length. Others, knowing better its power, have remained silent, or conveyed the fact of their ownership by only the obliquest means. These are the ones, it may be, who have inadvertently allowed the story that the Book is no real book at all, but only an idea of such, a dream. So it has happened, in any case, that it has vacillated, through recent centuries, between substance and rumour, theory and fact, sometimes disappearing almost entirely, sometimes assuming, if we are to believe the rare accounts, such tangible form that you could break a head with it, thump it on a cockroach or (most outrageously of all) be painted or photographed, holding the Book in your hands, a thing at once of infinite dimension, of staggering size, and yet 'no more than two inches thick, a work of but two hundred pages, sewn untitled between crudest boards, having for illustration only the entrance hole of a worm, who subsequently departs the text at about the hundredth page'.

Or so, at least, we might imagine Sir Humphrey Rivers writing some time in his later years, when eschatalogy had all but replaced philology in his mind, and he could afford some levity at words' expense. It had not been so when, nearly forty, he had stumbled from the jungles of Ecuador, clutching a thing wrapped in giant liana leaves, convinced that he had found, in the rubble of a monastery, the seed itself of all literature, and from then on guarded it as if it were his life.

One can only guess what went on in that ruined place, how Rivers found it, how long he stayed – a place overrun by jungle, the books in its enormous library fallen from the broken shelves, already disintegrating into humus, their remaining pages thick with mould, their spines and leather bindings eaten by slaters, their texts, once set laboriously, letter by letter, by printers in Lyons, Antwerp, Lima, Madrid, now swollen and discoloured by the potent interminglings of ink and vegetation, and in the centre of it all, a few books in all appearance scarcely touched, any and all of which a reader might have taken, and only one of which he did.

It seemed to him, this book, or came to seem, the sum of all that he had ever known or even fleetingly desired, a book as complex and as various, as terrible and as bounteous as the mind itself, with the same dark passages, the same grand vistas, the same half-suspected guilts and secrets, a book that held all possibilities of thought, all certainty and all perplexity. Not within one reading, it was true, but whenever it was reapproached, a new world opened: characters had changed, events were seen from new perspectives, discourse was deeper or more difficult than before, with unsuspected subtleties, unthought-of implications. As dense as a tropic jungle, as ornate as a cathedral, one never stepped into the same text twice: always there were found new themes, new symbols, readings never yet imagined, always there were vital passages completely missed before, as if, even while resting undisturbed – the library locked, the key safely upon Sir Humphrey's person – the book had been changing, parts of it dying, others growing, seeding anew, the words themselves fertilizing their own rich undersoil, more like a forest than a thing of paper. Sometimes, indeed, bending close to its pages, it seemed that one could even catch faint odours of decay, or soft, delicious perfumes of new growth, the scent of leaf-mould, the damp, cold exhalation of a newly opened tomb.

This story, however, is not of Sir Humphrey, but of the Book itself. Apart from his journal, some account of his travels, and the late, short *History of Gardens*, the knight did not take up the pen, for all his interest in literature. The true and proper history of the Book in our own culture starts, instead, with a nephew, a courtier poet, and from thence descends, in erratic hops and dramatic, downward slides, one of the most cluttered and eccentric family trees until the point where, like the worm, it departs altogether from the page, only to appear on quite another for three further generations. The pattern repeats itself almost until the present age. Four clans, at least, at different times are dominated by the book. He who could trace it would find, bobbing conspicuously in its wake, not only one of the language's greatest philosophers, but one of our finest playwrights, our greatest essayist, a celebrated pamphleteer, the great Romantic aesthetician, a poetess, a novelist, and a whole, small galaxy of versifiers, satirists, chroniclers of the bizarre and strange. It is a record unequalled in our literature, and yet, so thickened and so tangled has each family tree become, so unappealing to the covetous has always been the book's appearance – so often, that is to say, has lawful inheritance given way before affection, fortune, love of writing – that the observance of this passage, brilliant as so many of its stations are, has as yet defied philologist and genealogist alike.

Possession, moreover, has never been sufficient precondition for such flowering. Over and again, sometimes for decades, the Book has lain dormant. Some libraries, it seems, provide more fertile soil than others. The record of its power, its genius, influenced as it may have been by fortune, blood or friendship, is in fact also the record of one particular event, albeit in several variations.

The young philosopher, let us say, unaware as yet that that is what he will become, returns from hunting or some dalliance in the capital and, after eating, after entertaining friends, retires to the library, to spend some warm and quiet moments with a familiar volume, only to find it altered inexplicably. The poet, reaching for Ovid, checking a quotation, finds there a word that he had not remembered and, reading on, discovers his copy – a translation – remarkably yet beautifully corrupt, the names confused, events misplaced, the text itself reproducing uncannily the transformations of its subject.

Such incidents cannot be ignored; their pathology is swift. The rearrangement of words, the alteration of sentences, the volatility of thought and narrative increases as the owner nears its source, the volumes closest to it altered sometimes almost unrecognizably by this proximity. Sooner rather than later he or she suspects the Book, and from then on, for the chosen or susceptible, their fate has come upon them, the seeds of mutability and transgression entering their minds, their blood-streams, affecting all that they do or write thereafter. The Book, that is, takes root in certain places like a tropic vine, becomes established like a mould, a parasite, taking its different forms dependent upon the nature of its host.

In the library of the poetess, for example, the parts of speech change function, verbs migrate to points of action grammar never offered them. In the non-sense that ensues, giving effort and time, new kinds of sense emerge, language develops sinews, muscles unknown before. It seems to her that now it closely wraps a world of sense, of feeling, that hitherto it only gestured to, or rested on like dried mud on a river-bed, or plaster cracking from a wall.

To the dramatist, the Book is something else again. Although we know he had it – willed it to his friend – nowhere does he mention it, and yet, reading his plays, we know for him it was a World of Worlds, a great, enchanted forest in which, straying from glade to glade, he met character upon character whose life and situation all but consumed him – each clearing, as it were, a stage, another country, a tragedy or comedy only awaiting him to see and set it down.

The secret, it seems, is not in Law, but in some growing thing. The mathematicians, the physicists of texts will never quite discover it. The almost infinite permutation of a finite alphabet, a known and predetermined language, cannot suffice as explanation when the letters, the very words themselves are rotting, growing, sending out fibrous, re-rooting tendrils that in turn adapt in unpredictable new ways within the sentences that house them. I have called the Book a mould, a parasite, taking on its different forms depending upon the nature and condition of its host – but could it be that *we* are parasites, the Book the host, or that we both exist in some as yet unenvisioned symbiosis, the range of our mutually dependent forms as limitless as the natural world itself?

But I speak as if the Book, through all its changes, were in essence still the same. Nowadays this, like its whereabouts, is not so clear. With the vast dissemination of knowledge in our time, with the extent and intensity of our scholarship, enough about the Book is known, or at least suspected, that there are now, I'm sure, many hundreds, if not thousands, scattered about the globe, who pore over the pages of newspapers and journals, or browse continuously the bookshops, looking for its tell-tale signs. Something has happened. Perhaps it is merely a symptom of our era – our fragmentation and our restlessness, our individual truth-seeking – or perhaps it is that the Book itself has somehow changed more radically than ever before: that, steeped too long in the one library somewhere, between the first and second wars, the volumes it affected have themselves become contagious and, distributed, now threaten us with a strange, global infestation of infoliating sentences, texts that never finish, words that have lost their old stable meanings, or, mirroring our discontent, never quite stay where we have put them, but shift about listlessly, as if seeking a new grammar, an utterly different order.

The City of Labyrinths

It is doubtful that you would ever reach Icara; indeed, it is doubtful whether its founders ever intended that you should. Not only is the city itself a warren of scarcely credible proportions, but the routes one must follow to it are amongst the strangest ever contrived. Highways there are aplenty; one can begin on a well-marked thoroughfare from any of the major towns in the surrounding provinces; but before a great many miles have passed the problems of direction and incertitude begin. One comes to a crossroads, or a fork in the highway, and it is not immediately apparent which choice one should make. And then, whichever alternative is taken, one finds, before many more miles have passed, one's highway becoming a road and, that road forking, the fork taken becoming an unsealed track, a country lane, a rutted and muddy cowpath. By the time one had expected to be entering the city, one is driving instead at a snail's pace to avoid pot-holes or, sandwiched between high, unclipped hedges, waiting impatiently for a shepherd to manoeuvre his flock into an inconceivable single file so that one might pass.

It is a test, of course; how could it not be? The faint-hearted – or faint-headed – soon try to retrace their steps, while the temperamentally sympathetic, much to their surprise, begin at last to find the situation easing. As if they had in fact only taken a complicated detour, the appropriate signs reappear, roads widen, surfaces improve, and one finds oneself, as one had thought one always would be, on a major highway, heading towards a major town: Icara, in the province of Atria.

The maps perhaps might help, but rarely do. The problems I describe defy cartographers and yet, as it may not surprise you to hear, are also strangely dependent upon them. The confusions, the necessary ambiguities of the journey, are only heightened by the existence there, on paper, of clear, published evidence to the contrary. But let one try to get there!

An aerial view, if one could get one, would show the trick to be simple enough. Icara conducts its business with the world not by clear and simple thoroughfares, but rather as the blood gets to and from the heart, to understand which statement we need only imagine the highways one sets out upon as major arteries, steering their cargo of fresh, bright blood, and those one reaches at last, if one persists, as veins which ferry an older, darker liquid back. And in between, carrying the blood from one system to the other, is that perplexing, ill-signposted network of arterioles and capillaries, branching ever smaller and smaller until a point where the process reverses and the million tiny channels become now tributaries to greater and greater streams.

And when one at last arrives at the heart, one finds that it is a walled city, ancient yet modern, called by many the City of Labyrinths because, for almost a thousand years, its citizens, restrained by those walls and by the impossibility – so limited are they by their small plateau – of ever extending beyond them, have built in upon themselves in such a manner as has engendered the most intricate of architecture. It is a city not only of narrow, zig-zagging lanes and alleyways, of streets barely wide enough for bicycles to pass, but also of giddy, winding staircases, where the horizontal ingenuity transposes to the vertical, where houses have been built upon houses, rooms upon rooms, and premises that might once have been at street level now find themselves considerably beneath it or, conversely, far above. As much a place of convoluted basements as of attics, of subterranean as of aerial passageways, moreover, for generations now no one looking at the city on its heights has been able to tell where true mountain ceases and the human work begins, so riddled – so warren-like with tunnels and interconnected cellars – has the original plateau become.

Small wonder then that, turning necessity into an art form, Icara became, at some far point in its long past, a city also of private and deliberate labyrinths, where rich men vied for the most confusing establishment, with the most unexpected doors and passages, the most misleading of façades. Small wonder, too, that it became a place of secrets, a place of refuge and incarceration, a place of treasures hidden from the public eye.

But rich men do not always live longer than poorer, and certainly not for ever. Their estates are distributed, their dynasties collapse. Even the most ornate and elaborate of Icara's houses have since been subdivided, and now often shelter many families where once they housed just one. Some have been taken over by the market areas, while as many others now accommodate sections of the city's extensive, nightmare bureaucracy. One can get as lost now paying one's water bill as might once a guest at a party of one of the city's great families.

Inhabitants of Icara, this is to say, are used to finding that the normal surfaces of their lives can give unexpectedly upon mazes, that the renovation of a wall, say, or a cabinet, can reveal an unsuspected doorway, which might lead, yes, into a neighbour's house, but which might also disclose basements, corridors, entire apartments that have long lain derelict. Some, indeed, have suggested that there is a whole city within the visible Icara, a ghost city of neglected and forgotten labyrinths into which, as often by design as accident, an unknown number of citizens go yearly missing, never to be seen again.

No one, in any case, can be truly certain of the full extent even of their own property. The files in the titles office are themselves a labyrinth of inestimable proportions. Builders and renovators, I have heard, would rather change their trades than seek council approval. For all the efforts of recent, enlightened administrations, and for all our marvellous advances in information systems, there is no index, no one person who could give any reliable idea of the full size and complexity even of one of the city's own buildings, let alone of a city block.

There are dungeons beneath the court house, catacombs below the cathedral, sewers underneath them all (leading to the famous Sluice, one hundred feet below the Ghetto wall), but these, like so many other systems in Icara, so intrude upon one another that only the most daring or avaricious, the most

desperate or foolhardy will ever enter them. Horizontal labyrinths, vertical labyrinths, subterranean and rooftop mazes – the
citizens of Icara become, in the long run, only too used to a kind
of bizarre miscegeny whereby one barely comprehended structure can bisect another. Even on the most frequently performed
of errands, one can, if one's concentration lapses, find oneself
exhausted, several hours and streets away from one's original
destination. Few, then, could be surprised to find Icara famed
for its intrigue, or to hear that it was once a dreaded centre for
the Inquisition. How convenient Icara's little streets and alleys,
its shadowy courtyards and piazzas for the disposal of a rival,
and how readily into such can, even now, a band of robbers or
assailants melt away!

Responding to its bizarre environment – perhaps made by it as
it has made it – the collective mind of Icara has become an
impressive combination of the vicious and the receptive, of the
suspicious and the flexible, as if hyper-aware not only of the
dangers, but also of the promise of the labyrinth. Not only does
one find, when speaking with its citizens, that characteristic
sentence in which phrases, clauses, subjects multiply until one
forgets where one began, or how one might identify an ending if
it came – not only does one become thus quickly used to a
strange, meandering discourse in which, as often as not, one
finds oneself a great distance from original premisses, discussing
subjects or entertaining positions one had never thought to hold
– but even in oneself, if one stays long enough, one begins to see
how, in this place, mistrust of surfaces, a lack of confidence in
present realities, inflower to become a fearlessness, an enterprise
in the face of the unknown. These people may seem, at first, the
most suspicious and elusive in the world, but they are also
amongst the least complacent. Evil and discovery, violence and
creation have become close neighbours here, and even that
fundamental dependence upon material things, so characteristic
of the race, has changed, ready as the people of Icara must always
be to find themselves separated, not only from each other, but
from the known surroundings, the familiar possessions that,
elsewhere, might give to life its meaning.

I write, of course, as an outsider. A native of the city might give a very different assessment. So too, not all who travel there will wish to stay as long as I. But such is the influence of the place that even 'go' and 'stay' have unsuspected meanings. There are, in any case, at least two main ways out of Icara. The first is to retrace one's steps as best one can, down from the plateau onto one of the highways and thence, through the aforementioned intricacies of delta and recombination, eventually to the city from which one came. The second is to stay. Slowly, surely, the City of Labyrinths becomes something else, a place that, for all its unusual architecture, for all the Byzantine complexities of its design, is more like that from which one came than one would ever have thought possible.